To Meertha –
with good wishes

JH Burrell

lives near us, at the
beach, 226 Warren Ave

12-2011
Yankee Bk Store
Plymouth

Last Summer
at the Compound

Disclaimer
This book is a work of fiction. Although the geography is real, any connection to people living or dead is purely coincidental.

Copyright ©2011 J H Bartlett
All rights reserved.
ISBN: 1466285826
ISBN 13: 9781466285828

Dedicated with love and thanks to the family

The Lloyd Family

John m. Catherine buys Plymouth property in 1908. They have one son:

Harold m. Margaret. They have three sons:

    John (b1933) (opts out of compound)

(the following take part last summer at the compound)

    Parker, (b1935) m Priscilla. They have three children:
- **Helen** m Bernard deRussey, (2 unnamed children)
- **Ben** m Natalie Canova (2 unnamed children, one on the way)
- **Sarah** engaged to Bob Meyers

    Paul (b1938) m Kitty. They have two children:
- **Ann** m Dr. Frank Moran (3 children: Maggy plus 2 unnamed)
- **Harry** about to marry Peter

*Ruling generation

Last Summer at the Compound

J H Bartlett

One

They were sitting on the porch talking about weather, the family's favored safe topic. When his sister appeared out of the fog, Ben stood up to greet her with an exaggerated continental kiss on each cheek. "Helene ma chère, comment ça va?"

"Fine till I heard your lousy accent. Hello Ann, give me a hug and tell all."

"No gossip, no politics, no sex until this damn meeting is over," Ben said. "And I might add, just one drink. We're having gin and tonics. I'll get you one."

"Good, thanks." Helen lowered her large bottom into a white plastic chair. "I suppose I should lose weight before I break all the new chairs."

"You look great," Ann said. "I'm so glad to see you. Are the kids all right? Being here must feel strange to them."

"Not really. They talk all year about life in America, as they call their visits here, and we reminisced on the plane and at your mother's last night. You know we stayed with her in Boston so we could meet Harry at Logan and drive down together. He had to take an afternoon flight from Washington. Apparently his assignment to Syria has been cancelled and he was held up at State Department meetings."

"Where IS Harry?"

"Unpacking and playing with the kids. He couldn't wait to see them . . . I couldn't wait to get away from them. They've all been warned, I gather, that they are to stay at the Big House while we have the annual meeting."

"Ben has taken care of it all. Older and younger generations plus spouses and other non–essential personnel are to be wined and dined at the Big House tonight. My mother is in charge."

"Where's Sarah?" Helen asked.

"She'll be a little late and will have to leave early to pick up Bob at Town Hall."

By the time Harry and Sarah arrived, they were through their drinks and being eaten by mosquitoes. They chatted while moving inside to the screened-in porch/dining room, careful not to say anything personal or controversial. It wasn't easy. Harry had big news, which he'd told Helen as she unpacked. Ben looked anxious and Sarah was on edge.

The great grandfather of this group had bought the property in Plymouth in the early 1900's. There was an old fishing shack on it, which he either expanded or tore down (stories differ). In any case, he built a summer house with porches all around and a guest house. Over the garage was an apartment for his driver and cook couple. The Portable (so called because it was a prefab house, one of the first) was added in the early 1930's when his only child, Harold, married. Harold and Margaret had three boys, John, Parker and Paul, who eventually also married and produced eight children in all. These families spent most of every summer of their growing up years in the Compound. Cousins played together, running from one house to another for meals or sleeping. Cousins or siblings, they hardly knew which was which. When his children were teenagers, John divorced, moved to California and never returned. The present generation didn't know whether there was some incident or whether he just decided to live a new life. Now there are five family units in the present so-called ruling generation left for summer compound living: the families of Helen, Ben and Sarah (children of Parker and Priscilla); and the families of Ann and Harry (children of Paul and Kitty). Some years earlier the family lawyer drew up a contract setting out what is required of each family and what they get in return if they plan to spend time in the Compound.

"The annual meeting will come to order," Ben, sitting at the head of the dining room table, announced. This was hard for Helen. She hadn't seen the family for a year and needed to feel them out, talk to them, be with them. She hated having this meeting before she even finished unpacking. What was Ben thinking?

"First of all I want to say that I know if we don't do this meeting now and do it formally, we never will. And there actually are things we have to go over," said

4

Ben. "Second, I think we should vote on who will be chairman each year. I don't want to take a lot of shit from you guys and if someone else will take over, I'll happily pass the gavel."

"We appreciate your doing this, Ben, even though you are a puffed up bag of wind. No . . . seriously, carry on. I doubt anyone else wants the job, much less could do the job," said Harry.

"OK," said Ben. "If you're all agreed." And he spoke about expenses and repairs, taxes, balancing the books, schedules and assignments. Helen half listened. Beetles and mosquitoes were dive bombing into the screens. The outside light was surrounded by moths. The fog horn blew. Paintings by the children, collages of shells and dried seaweed fought for space on the inside wall of the porch. Some things were the same, thank goodness. She remembered elegant and slightly drunken dinner parties at this table. When she married Bernard she referred to her mother's tattered Julia Child cookbook. She was Mastering the Art of French Cooking right here in the run down cottage by the sea. She tarted up the house with Pierre Deux chintz, put another coat of paint on the furniture, geraniums in the window boxes, et voila, Provence on the rocky coast of Massachusetts. They would mix Bernard's colleagues from Harvard Business School with some of the local eccentrics and eat moules followed by gigot d'àgneau.

"So that's the year-end report," Ben concluded. "Now for some new business. We're pregnant."

"Oh Ben. Congratulations. When is she due?"

"Good god old man. That makes three in as many years. I thought Nat gave up Catholicism."

"It's not that. Ben's just oversexed."

"I thought we weren't going to discuss personal stuff till after the annual meeting," said Sarah. "Because I have something to say that pertains to the contract."

"As do I," said Harry.

"OK," said Ben. "But the pregnancy does affect the Compound contract, or at least I have an idea I want to bring up. I'll put my proposal off till hearing from Sarah and Harry. And you, too, Helen and Ann, since I've been doing all the talking."

Oh, boy, Helen thought. Here we go. "I have nothing to add," she said. "You're doing a great job, Ben."

"I second that," Ann said.

"You first, then Sarah," said Harry. "Is Bob going to make an honest woman of you?"

Bob Meyers was Sarah's latest flame. Bright, articulate, good looking, he is an environmental lawyer with a firm in Boston, but still lives with his large, loyal, loquacious family in a Victorian house in downtown Plymouth. He is on the Planning Board and a strong advocate of conservation and community preservation. Plymouth is suffering severe growing pains. Like a lovely virgin maiden, this old New England town is being raped and ravished by unrelenting and unrestrained development. Bob is outspoken and hardworking and has made as many enemies as friends and supporters. Sarah is in the latter two categories.

She blushed. "Well the subject has come up, but it's another issue I want to discuss at this meeting."

"Uh oh. This will mean that dear Sarah won't be satisfied doing her Compound time in the Portable in the fall. She'll soon be producing little ones and demanding equal share of the high season at the Big House."

"No. I'm afraid you've got it all wrong. What I want to say is that I think we ought to sell this place."

They were silent. Finally, Ben said, "I knew this was coming. She's been involved with the anti-nuke group and they have scared her shit-less." The rest of them were speechless.

"For one thing, clean up your language Ben," said Sarah. "And for another, I don't understand how you can bring a new child into the world living less than two miles from an aging nuclear power plant that at any moment could either blow up or be attacked by terrorists."

Oh damn, thought Helen. There goes my longed for gentle holiday at the old family compound. Her strategy regarding the power plant was to ignore it. It is around the point and out of sight from the Compound. Only when sailing off shore does it come into her line of vision and awareness. But she recognized that Sarah, involved in town affairs through Bob, couldn't help but be concerned.

Ann said, "Is it really serious Sarah? I mean are people in town worried? Is there some sort of report that documents the problems? I've read a little in the Boston papers, but there seem to be differing opinions."

"It's very serious. Even before Fukushima many of us were worried. Bob has been meeting with a group of nuclear physicists, former NRC officials among others. They have a number of concerns about the state of the plant. And all the spent fuel rods from previous years are languishing just down the road waiting to go to Yucca Mountain in Nevada. And it now turns out Yucca doesn't want them."

"Well, we're not going to sell out the Compound right now." said Ben. "It's a worthy topic to discuss, but let's put it on hold for a while."

"How can you say that Ben? The plant may blow at any minute. Do you have plans for evacuation? I know you Ben. You love all the business the plant spins off. You love the funds it gives to the hospital, the library, and the arts centre. It's bribery, dirty money winning over the hearts and minds of the townspeople."

"OK you two. Let's save it for later. I want to tell you my news," said Harry. "I'm getting married."

That shut them up.

"But I thought you said you were gay," said Ann.

"Ann, my dear, when the tree fell on Dad's head, I asked Mum if he'd been drinking before deciding to trim dead limbs. Do you know what she replied? 'Harry, dear, it was eleven in the morning.' I said to her, 'Mother, the time of day was not my question.'"

"What does that have to do with you getting married?" asked Ben.

"Ann's question was as irrelevant as Mum's answer to mine. That is, Dad used to drink at any time of day; I am gay and I am getting married."

8

"You mean you're marrying a man?" Ann asked.

"That's what I mean. I called the town clerk and we've set the date. Peter thinks it would be fun to have the ceremony on a party boat in the harbor and the clerk says that's fine. He said ever since Massachusetts allowed same sex marriages he's been performing ceremonies in some fascinating venues."

"Jesus Harry, are you trying to kill your mother?" Ben asked. "She's barely getting over the shock of your father's accident and is settling into some kind of a routine and now you're going to hit her with this."

"Look guys," Helen said. "I'm going to call the Big House to tell them we won't be down for supper. The grandparents and spouses can keep the kids down there for a while. We've got some talking to do. I'll get pizzas delivered. We've got plenty of beer, but I'm not cooking tonight."

This was the start of the summer of 2011. What a start. Usually, by the Fourth of July they were settled in and having a cookout on the banking. This year there was a feeling pulsing through the family that things were not right. The houses needed repairs, but that was nothing new. The family clung to the old ways as if with their taste for antiques, fix-up patching, and candlelight they could keep away the problems of modern life, which most of them seemed unable to cope with. Ben thought this was a sign of failure and predicted a downward slide into the swamp yankee class. He'd seen it happen with his friends. Friends born into old Boston families barely making it through college, not prepared for much of anything and unwilling to take a job beneath their idea of themselves, their houses falling down around them, their clothes, seedy and patched. Finally they would take some menial job (if they were lucky) and spend the rest of their lives talking about their prep schools or some past Harvard Yale game.

The house they were meeting in, the Portable, sits slightly higher than the other houses and back from the ocean cliff. Although it is on the most stable land in the Compound, it has settled and has a decided list to the east. Most windows do not close completely and none of the doors. The Lloyds have rigged up a sailing cleat and line to hold the bathroom door closed. There are three bedrooms, one bathroom, a living room, dining room and kitchen with a room off the kitchen. In the grandparents' generation that room off the kitchen was for the maid and in the parents', for the au pair. Now it's a storeroom with a washing machine. You walk right into the living room off the front patio, a raised patio made of cement, now cracked cement, painted some years gray, others, terra cotta. The screen door is serviceable and slams, though the open spaces around it allow in bugs of various families. There are three dilapidated wicker chairs on the porch with old cushions, an iron two-seater porch swing, and a table with four white plastic chairs. The living room has a grass rug on the painted floor, an overstuffed couch recently home to a mouse family, a few pull up chairs. A lobster pot has been brought in to use as a coffee table, fitted with a glass top so drinks don't tip. Kitty, empties the bureau drawers in the spring and lines them with lavender paper. She doesn't trust anyone else to do the job since she doesn't want mouse families destroyed. She pulls open drawers of mice with their nests made of pillow stuffing, toilet paper and whatever is on offer from the kitchen shelves. She takes those drawers to the woods in back of the house, where the dogs and cats are buried, and gently dumps them. She makes the beds while she's at it, with sheets and pillow cases of mismatched prints and stripes. Last spring she could be heard calling, here foxy, foxy, because Ben had told her he thought a den of foxes had moved in over the winter, or some other beasties with spore larger than mouse. She won't allow mouse poison, but does let moth balls be thrown around each fall at close-up time.

The view of the ocean is pretty good from the Portable, but it takes constant pruning and tree cutting or choke cherries, deadly nightshade and bittersweet block it out. That's how Paul lost his senses—cutting limbs and trees in front of the Portable. The previous October he had decided to clean up after a September hurricane with the power saw he'd been given for his birthday. A half fallen tree he was cutting fell the wrong way and hit him on the head. He now resides at Brewster House, the youngest and best looking inmate at Plymouth's favorite nursing home.

Sarah left the meeting, drove downtown and waited in front of Town Hall for Bob. People were standing in groups on the steps and landing, some of them she recognized—town meeting members, real estate lawyers, the local Nature Conservancy person. She hunkered down behind the wheel, not wanting to talk or even wave. Bob came out, shuffled past the others. He looked tired. But god he was handsome. Always decked out in blazer and chinos, white shirt and tie in spite of the local penchant at town hall for Red Sox baseball hats and Patriots sweat shirts.

"Thanks for picking me up. I was going to go over to the house and get Rebecca's car. Jesus what a meeting"

"What's going on?"

"We're hearing the Hazen Development Company proposal. The jerks want to build on the Nuclear power plant's buffer land. The company has been dealing with the power company people behind the scenes, offering them a good price. Can you imagine anyone even considering building, much less living in, houses that close to the plant?"

"Did you say anything?"

"Of course I did. You know me. I told them I thought they were crazy—the Hazen Company that is—and I told the Planning Board we shouldn't waste our time on such an idiot proposal. I got a lot of dirty looks. Nobody wants to face the truth. No, it's not really that. They just don't get it. Don't understand that it's all right to leave land as it is. It's OK to say no to developers. Town Hall thinks big money will come in from taxes on houses and the developers from out of town think big rich guys will want to live in McMansions next to a decrepit and failing nuclear power plant, or that they won't notice before they buy."

12

Sarah drove north along the harbor and took a left to get them back to Main Street. Bob talked on non-stop. The wonderful articulate talk she loved. But he was wearing himself out. She could see it in his face. Dark circles had appeared under his eyes. Town issues were going to kill him. He was passionate about protecting the beauty of the land and the history of the town and it hurt him to see the place overrun by developers. Walmart, MacDonalds, Dunkin Doughnuts and other chain stores and restaurants were slithering into town, bulldozers were crashing through woods and farms. Apple orchards and cranberry bogs were disappearing, while farmers made a killing selling out. Condos were being built along the harbor, gravel pits dug and mined. Plymouth land was disappearing to the highest bidder. They were either trucking it out as sand and gravel or desecrating it with housing developments, strip malls, and big box stores. They'd give them nice names like Colonial Place and Derbyshire Village, and create traffic studies to show there would be no congestion at all. They would talk about the tax base and all the new taxes that will come in from development; they'd talk about set-backs, roof lines, empty nesters, village centers, traffic taming, natural landscaping—all fine words to lull the sleeping town boards into thinking life in the town (and for themselves) will improve in every way. No mention was made of crowded schools, overworked police and fire departments, overwhelmed town departments struggling to keep up with licenses for dogs, births and deaths, complaints, traffic jams, snow plowing, road repairs. No. They would talk about new jobs, then bring in their own construction crews from elsewhere. They'd talk about business being good for the economy, then give the new companies tax incentives.

"Whoof, I'm beat," said Bob. "Where are we headed anyway?"

"Family confab. They're all going at it now. I dropped the bomb about selling out, but it was overshadowed by Harry's announcement. He's getting married."

"But I thought he is gay."

"As he said, what's that got to do with it."

"Oh yeah. I forgot the new law. So no reaction about selling off the Compound?"

"Ben suggested we table the motion."

"Good. Put it off. I hate to think of your family leaving that spot. There's so much history there. It's almost sacred ground."

"Well there will be nothing left of the sacred ground or of us if that power plant blows."

"I wish you wouldn't worry about it. I'm afraid I got you going in that direction. We may still be able to get it closed down and get those spent rods into a safe environment. Don't rush in and upset your family."

"Dammit Bob. You're always so nice and so reasonable. Well here we are. Home again, home again, jiggety jog. I've got to go finish up with the big five at the Portable. You non-essential personnel are having dinner at the Big House. I'll meet you there at about nine. We should be done by then. Hey look. You don't have to be here. You look really tired."

"I've been a little under the weather. Don't know what it is. I thought for a while I might have Lyme disease. But don't worry about it. I'd rather be here with your family than anywhere else. I'm going to take a quick dip first. My suit still on the peg?"

"I think so. Beware. It's low tide and cold. Don't freeze those gonads. They're too precious."

"For such a straight laced puritan girl, you're a pretty raunchy babe."

Sarah headed up to the portable and met Al's pizza truck on its way out.

Two

Kitty stood at the stove in the Big House kitchen, a glass of Chardonnay in one hand, mixing spoon in the other. Salt pork scraps were trying out in the iron skillet, turning brown, giving off fat. She removed the pieces of pork and added chopped onions to the grease, letting them cook slowly to become translucent before tipping the pan and pouring the onions and fat into the kettle with the chopped potatoes and clam broth. As these simmered she took a sip of her wine.

The Big House is about twenty feet from the edge of the cliff. They call the lawn between the house and the cliff the banking. The house has been moved back once already, sometime in the 1930's. The ocean eats away at the banking and carries the sand out to sea depositing it at the public beach. Landowners along the coast have tried everything to prevent erosion, but recently have all but given up because of stricter conservation laws and the realization that you can't fight Mother Nature, especially when she takes the form of a northeast storm. Nor'easters in New England are fierce and the Compound is perfectly sited to take the brunt of them. The storms, they say, always last three days. Three days of strong wind, high seas and rain. Three days of pulling out bread pans and aluminum pots from the kitchen cupboards to catch the leaks. Three days of battering winds that shake the pictures off the walls and force the Lloyds to stay inside to worry about their ten lobster pots and whether someone ought to go out to the mooring and pull in the dingy. The chairs on the porches slam against the walls. If they are lucky, they have remembered to bring in the cushions and the pots of geraniums.

And when the storm has passed, they go out on the banking and marvel at the calmness of the bi-polar ocean. They mop up windowsills and floors, remind each other that next time they will make sure all the upstairs windows are closed. The children go down to the beach to check for flotsam and jetsam, to untangle lines and collect colored lobster buoys. The parents will check on the damage to the banking, see whether erosion is threatening.

Things are changing, Kitty thinks as she cooks. Nothing stays the same, of course, she could accept that, but things are moving fast and in ways she can't understand. The next generation takes over. She wouldn't argue with that. Let them. Give up your hold on this place she told herself. The kids are doing fine. They'll make the right decisions. But why are they so mysterious and quiet. What is going on? Is there something I should be doing? Well, making chowder for the nonessentials may be the best contribution. Staring into space, she was absently looking out the window. Her eyes rested on the spot where Paul was crushed by the tree. No. Not going to think about that now.

Natalie came into view walking over from the garage apartment, the big wooden salad bowl propped against her hip as if it were a child, her belly large under her tee shirt. "Hi Aunt Kitt. Smells good here."

"You dear girl. That salad looks like a meal in itself. Do you think chowder, salad, bread and blueberry pie is enough for the troops?"

"Sounds fine to me. The kids won't eat much. They've been grabbing stuff from the fridge all afternoon. Amazing how they pick right up again each summer without missing a beat."

"I know and I love it. It's good for children to race around in and out of houses with no adult supervision. A rare commodity these days. We must cherish it and thank our lucky stars for this Compound. How is the French contingent doing?"

"They were a bit shy at first. But you know Lizzie. She's leading the gang as only she can do, organizing games, making sure all the kids feel included."

"What is she now. fourteen?"

"I believe so. I suppose in a year or so she'll be into boys and we'll lose her. But she certainly is the glue that holds the cousins together. I'll bet she will have a theatrical performance ready before long."

"Natalie. Can you tell me what's going on? There's a feeling I have, an aura in the Compound that disturbs me."

"I'm not sure what it is or if it is but I know what you mean. I suppose they'll let us in on the secrets, if there are any, after the big deal so-called annual meeting. But what about you? How are you getting along? You look great but I'm sure it's not easy."

"I was down at Brewster House this afternoon. They are so good with him. And they told me how often you visited during the winter. Thank you. It means a lot to me. I'm not sure Paul knows one way or another, but I think, and you must too, that we should assume he knows we're there and that he appreciates it in certain deep areas of his brain and heart."

"Well he's an easy guy to visit. He always smiles and somehow that makes things pleasanter all around."

"I know. It's as if that tree froze a smile on his face when it fell on him. And, flirting with the girls! Apparently the nurses have to hold him back. But the old girls—the inmates—love his attention. He makes them feel young and desirable again. I guess that's the life force at work. The romancing and mating game never stops until you're dead. And then, as Woody Allen asks, 'Is there sex after death?'"

"Hey you two beauties." Bob stood at the screen door dripping. "Could you hand me a towel. I'm going to take a shower outside if it's OK."

"Bobby! What a treat to see you. How did you get here?" Kitty asked.

"Sarah dropped me off before heading back to the annual meeting. I just took a plunge in the icy wine dark sea." He took the towel and headed for the shower. The shower was enclosed on the sides and open to the sky above. He took off his bathing suit and lathered up.

"Peek a boo. We see you." The kids giggled and pointed from the second floor window looking down on him.

He looked up at their beaming faces. "Hey you naughty children. That's a no-no and you know-know it. Go play in traffic." When he lowered his head to look for the soap, he was suddenly dizzy. He could barely stand up. What the hell!?? His legs were like jelly. He held on to the wooden towel rack and wrapped the towel around his waist. He was shivering and shaking. His legs gave out and he crumpled to the wood slatted shower floor. When he came to, he pounded his fist against the cedar walls and tried to yell.

"Hey Bob. Are you OK?"

"Lizzie. I need some help. Run and get Sarah."

"I'm not supposed to bother them. I'll get someone else." When he opened his eyes he saw Natalie standing over him – a shimmering vision whose face he could barely make out.

"God, Bob. What is it?"

"I don't know. Maybe I just need a drink and some food." Natalie ran around the house to the front porch. Frank was splayed out on the wicker chaise longue looking out to sea, sipping a rum and tonic. He roused himself reluctantly. He was not amused by these family crises which seemed to be cropping up with more and more regularity. Damn it. He liked to come home from the hospital, have his drink, say good night to the children (just his own children, not this army of cousins), open a bottle of wine and have a nice quiet dinner with Ann. The Compound for him was something he put up with for Ann's sake and something he used as a bedroom on summer weekends when he spent the better part of each day in his boat off shore, fishing or just floating around.

When he saw Bob, Frank instinctively and immediately reverted into his doctor persona. Bob was crumpled on the floor of the shower stall. Frank took his pulse and checked other vital signs.

"I'm taking him to the hospital. Get Kitty to help me put him in my car. You shouldn't be lifting Natalie.

"I'm OK. Good peasant stock. I always work right up to the birth."

Lizzie ran to the Portable followed by the pack of cousins. "Aunt Sarah . . ."

"Lizzie. We TOLD you – all of you – we are not to be disturbed.

"But Bob is sick and Dad is taking him to the hospital." She was crying, theatrically.

"Oh my God." Sarah rushed out and got in her car.

"What is happening to me?" Bob asked Frank. I've never been sick a day in my life. What is it?"

Frank assured him he would be fine. He was probably just stressed. He thought to himself that he would suggest at the hospital that they get fluids in and do blood work. Frank was a cardiologist attached to Mass General Hospital. He would have to tread carefully with the local doctors on staff here.

He knew all about egos and territory in the medical world. But he was concerned. Bob's symptoms didn't make sense. He was fine one minute, a strong healthy vital young man, and the next minute he collapses. No strength in his limbs. Low pulse, pale, dizzy. It was too sudden. He wanted to make sure the local doctors understood the seriousness.

Sarah's mind was racing as she drove to the hospital. She had seen Bob wasn't in top form when she picked him up at Town Hall. His color was wrong. The weekend before they had talked about the town and she had told him what she had heard. Cabals had formed in Town Hall and the Hazen Corporation was using any and every trick in the book to get its development over the hurdles and through the permitting process. Planning Board, Zoning Board, Conservation Commission. All these groups needed massaging. Developers needed friends within Town Hall to shepherd their projects through the hoops. If they were lucky, town staff would prepare the various volunteer boards, commissions and committees and convince them to take their word for it, convince them that they, as professionals, had read through all the rules and regulations and that the project would comply with state and federal laws. This was a big one in the works, the land surrounding the nuclear power plant, land that had been put aside originally to build a second power plant and when that was rejected by the town, was to be left as open space to serve as a buffer zone around the present plant. Hazen Corporation, the largest developer on the east coast was negotiating with the current owners of the power plant to buy seventy five acres of the property where they proposed to build twenty large houses all with views of the ocean and with clever landscaping of tall trees and bushes to conveniently hide the power plant from sight. Bob was horrified and didn't hold back his disdain and disgust to tell everyone the town was crazy to even consider this proposal. This land, he said, should stay in open space so that the citizens of Plymouth could visit the area and take in the view. Remains of a Wampanoag encampment had been discovered on the property. It was not beyond the realm of possibility that Indians were at this very spot looking out to sea when the Mayflower sailed by in the 1600's. Bob and his supporters were working to have the area protected and put on the Registry of National Historic Monuments. The Smithsonian had expressed interest. He just needed time to get a proposal together. Another reason for not building houses on the property was that should there be a problem at the power plant, or even a perception of a problem – a false alarm – the evacuation of an expanded population close to the plant in Area A would clog the roads yet further than now predicted. Already people were making snide remarks about the evacuation plan that had been put in place and endorsed by the Nuclear Regulatory Commission. People could see it just wouldn't work. Older citizens in town were saying they would sit tight, keep their cars off the roadways and let the younger generation get out if they could.

Bob's position on the Hazen proposal made sense and he had support. Unfortunately it was silent and passive, not the active support he needed. People were either busy with their day to day lives or preferred not to think about an end of the world type situation. Even after Fukushima they did not spend a lot of time thinking about the aging structure and about what would happen if a terrorist should bomb the power plant or if the plant should explode because of human error, or if there was leakage from the spent rods, now stored temporarily and insecurely waiting for removal out of town, removal that showed less and less chance of happening since there was no other place, seemingly, on the planet that wanted to store the rods. The problem was too big, too unsolvable, for the public to grasp. It was simpler to put heads in the sand and hope everything would turn out all right.

Inertia played into the hands of the Hazen Corporation. They looked to make a quick buck (billions of bucks) selling their fancy big houses and then leave town before the yuppy buyers caught wind of the problems or sight of the power plant. Hazen officials were not happy with this young rabble rouser, Bob Meyers, who was making trouble for them in Town Hall. Sarah's friend, Julie, who works in Town Hall had overheard the Hazen group taking about Bob and about the money it was costing them each day the building was held up. They needed to get their shovels into the ground and get under way. Their loans were large. She even heard one of them say, "We gotta get rid of this guy."

Three

The annual meeting had dispersed. Harry, Ann and Helen sat around for a while after Sarah left, drinking from the jug of red wine and nibbling pizza crusts. Ben had gone down to join Natalie at the Big House and to find out what had happened to Bob.

Ann asked Helen about her life in Paris. It's wonderful, she lied. "Pretty hard not to love Paris. My little business is going surprisingly well. Who'd have thought that American food would be fashionable in France. We have a small but elegant clientele. People who want something different. Le Brunch is a big hit."

"It's unbelievable. Good for you for coming up with the idea. What does Bernard think?"

"Well, he, of course, set up the whole business plan and he continues to oversee the finances. He thinks we ought to expand. Set up franchises in Lyon and Avignon and maybe London and Amsterdam. I don't know. It's a lot of work and we don't get to see much of each other as it is."

"Is he coming over this summer?" "No. He's tied up with some business deal. I'll tell you all about it later. Jet lag's beginning to hit and I'm looking forward to a nice bed and the sound of lapping waves to put me to sleep. You really don't mind my bunking in with you tonight at the Big House?"

"Hell no. I'm paying Lizzy to baby sit the girls here and leaving Buster with them for security."

"Buster's still alive? He must be ancient."

"Yep. He's still kicking, but just barely. He's a good watchdog, though, and the kids always feel safe when he's in the house with them at night. The boys have put up the tent in the orchard. How long they last is yet to be seen. But Natalie has turned the garage into a den. She calls it the pig pen – with old couches and beds lining the walls. They can crawl in there if things get scary outside. And she and Ben will be right upstairs."

Sarah parked near the emergency entrance and went in. No sign of Bob or Frank.

"Hey Sarah. What's up?" It was Rebecca, Bob's sister.

"Where's Bob?"

"What do you mean? Is he here in the hospital?"

"Frank brought him in about fifteen minutes ago."

"I just came on duty. What's the matter? step on a nail, poison ivy?"

"We don't know. Apparently he was unconscious. According to the kids. I wasn't with him."

"That doesn't sound good. Especially with Bob. He's healthy as a horse. Was it an accident?"

"I just don't know. Let's find him."

Rebecca checked the computer and saw that Bob had been rushed right through to intensive care. She began to panic. She and Bob were just a year apart and were the young team in their large family: seven kids and they were the youngest two. Aaron, the next closest in age was four years older and the four others went up in steps of one year apart. Rebecca and Bob were afterthoughts and were left pretty much to their own devises growing up. It had taken Rebecca a while to get used to Sarah. At first she didn't like her at all. The Meyers were townies and Jewish; the Lloyds, summer people and lapsed Episcopalians. But she finally admitted to herself that she would take a dim view of any one Bob chose.

"Come on Sarah. I know where he is." Rebecca got someone to cover for her at the desk and led Sarah through the swinging doors and down the hallway to the intensive care intake unit. Rebecca was greeted by everyone. She had worked at the hospital since she was fourteen, starting as a candy-striper. Now a beautiful woman of thirty, people were amazed she hadn't been snapped up by one of the young doctors. She loved her career and had advanced to assistant head nurse.

Bob lay on a gurney asleep or unconscious. An intravenous drip was attached to his left arm. Frank was talking to Ted Rushfield, the doctor on duty. Rebecca, in her capacity as nurse, went over to get in on their conversation. Sarah sat on the bed and held Bob's hand. "Can you hear me, Bob. Are you OK? We're all here with you. Hang in there. You'll be fine. Just need some nourishing. Some antibiotics or something. I love you Bob. Can you hear me? Squeeze my hand if you can." Nothing. But the heart monitor bleeped steadily. That must be a good sign.

Sarah had met Bob two years earlier at a beach conservation fund raiser at the Yacht Club. All the usual suspects, her mother had said as they walked into the party that was already in full swing. A true melting pot had taken place in town. Families had intermarried and ethnic lines were hazy and not strictly drawn. Sarah had once overheard the father of a Boston friend commenting about the elevation of Kevin McGonagle to chairman of the Board of the Boston Symphony, "They used to press our trousers and now they're wearing them." There was little of that tiresome WASP snobbism in Plymouth. And you could have found the same variety of people as were at this gathering at a chamber of commerce meeting; only those people would be involved in real estate, construction, banking and business, instead of tree hugging. There would be the same spread of different backgrounds you could read by surnames supporting development as supporting conservation: Italians, Portugese, Brazilians, Germans, English, Irish, blacks, Indians. As the local justice of the peace recently said, "When it comes to marriages ethnicity, color, race and religion don't concern people anymore. But you won't see a Democrat marrying a Republican."

Her mother, as soon as she was spotted, was surrounded by old friends. Sarah went up to the bar for a glass of wine. The young female bartender filled a plastic cup to the brim and overflowing. As Sarah turned away from the bar some spilled on the guy behind her.

"Oops. Sorry. My cup runneth over."

"Many's the slip twixt cup and lip? Don't worry. This jacket's ready for a cleaning anyway. Bob Meyers." He held out his hand.

"Sarah Lloyd," she replied, shaking his hand. "Are you from Plymouth?"

"I moved back last year after five years in Washington. So I'm a bit out of it. I haven't lived here since I went away to college. What about you?"

"Summer people. I live in Boston most of the time."

"Ah yes. The Lloyds. Your family place is down beyond Berts."

"That's the one." Sarah and Bob discovered they were both attached to environmental organizations. They retreated to the edge of the room to play do you know and make snide remarks about politically correct politicians and well heeled intellectuals who would support any good environmental cause but wouldn't, for instance, hear of a windmill where they might see it from their sailboats.

"I'm taking off." Priscilla tapped Sarah's shoulder. "My feet are killing me.'"

"Mum. This is Bob Meyers. He's a lawyer for the Nature Conservancy."

"Nice to meet you. Keep up the good work." She launched into a description of ways Canada was dealing with sprawl, the energy crisis and global warming and how her particular town in Ontario was managing growth issues.

"OK Mum. Let's go. It was good talking with you Bob."

Bob called the Big House the next morning. Lizzie raced over to the guest house. "Telephone, Aunt Sarah. It's a man!!"

Rebecca walked over and stood next to the bed. She took Bob's hand. "They can't figure out what the hell's wrong," she said to Sarah. "They rushed the blood work through. It showed a slight possibility of Lyme Disease, but nobody's ever seen Lyme present this suddenly and there's no tick bite mark. They asked me if there were any signs earlier this week of problems. But Bob and I have been ships passing in the night with me on the night shift here and him off to a site visit or to Boston early. What about you? Have you noticed anything unusual?"

Sarah, completely distraught, looked up at Rebecca. "I don't know. But he seemed a bit tired looking this past month, off and on. I thought he was just exhausted by all the crap he's fighting here in town on top of his work in Boston. What are they going to do?"

"We're trying to keep him stable, pumping a cocktail of antibiotics and nourishment into his body. Frank is calling colleagues at Mass General to see if they can weigh in on the possibilities. It could be that he picked up a rogue virus. God knows there are enough of them roaming around the globe."

"What do you mean? Killer bees, swine flu, mad cow disease?"

Frank came over to the bed to tinker with the tubes and feel Bob's head and take his pulse. He maintained that in spite of all the technical advances for reading a patient's state of health, there also needed to be intuition generated by being with the patient, touching, smelling, looking and listening.

Bob opened his eyes and smiled at his sister and Sarah. "I'm sure causing a lot of trouble here. What happened?"

"That's what we're trying to figure out," Frank said. "Now that you're with us, tell me everything you can about what you did and ate today and if you have energy, go back to the time when you first felt off your game."

"I haven't done or eaten anything unusual today. Cup of coffee and donuts on the way to the train this morning. Roast beef sandwich and milkshake at Joe and Nemos for lunch. Coke and candy bar at South Station at five to hold me through the Planning Board meeting. Glass of lemonade at the meeting. I don't remember any of the clients I was with or anyone in the office sneezing or throwing up. What can I tell you? I felt a little dizzy two weeks ago but it passed. Then again last week. I was nauseous and ached in my joints but nothing too serious. I don't . . ."

He closed his eyes. Frank checked the heart and pulse monitor.

"I want to get him to Mass General," he told Rebecca. There are people there who have had more experience with these off the charts cases. I think they'll diagnose and prescribe more accurately and quickly. This boy's very sick and we need to move fast. Use your clout and convince the staff that we've got to move him."

Four

Ann wandered down from the Portable, staggering slightly. Three gin and tonics under her belt, plus wine was too much. She knew that and also that the pizza didn't do as much absorbing as it might have. It was dark. She tripped on a root but caught herself before falling on her face and continued feeling her way along until she saw the kitchen lights of the Big House.

"Where's Frank?" She asked Kitty, Ben and Harry, who were sitting in the living room.

"Still at the hospital with Bob. You know how they back up at the emergency room on weekends."

"He'll be furious," said Ann. "But he's always careful not to throw his weight around. Knowing him, he'll be quietly waiting their turn and meanwhile the bashed and bleeding will be triaged in before them. Damn. Too bad this had to happen on our first night together. What's wrong with Bob anyway?"

"Nobody knows. He collapsed in the shower."

"I was just telling everyone about the wedding," said Harry.

"Yeah. He dropped that bomb," Ben said.

"Well, I think it's wonderful," said Kitty. "He and Peter have made a commitment and aren't afraid to act on it. I like Peter. Always have. Also he'll be a good partner for a foreign service officer, I would think, being a reporter. I assume his career is mobile and can often be in the same country or nearby."

"Thanks, Mum. It's true. He will stay on with the paper for a while, but he really wants to be an independent writer."

"My god! You're something, mother," Ann said. "We thought you didn't even know he was gay. There are plenty of people who flip out when they find their kids are gay."

"I'm not plenty of people and I'm not some old curmudgeon. Paul and I have always been proud of Harry, as proud of him as of you, Ann. And we talked over the possibility that he might be gay. Obviously, he wasn't going to play football for Harvard. And we adored watching him in the Hasty Pudding shows. But we didn't say anything. We waited for him to make an announcement, if an announcement was to be made."

"I'm only sorry I didn't get a chance to talk with Dad before the accident," Harry said. "I thought he was disappointed in me because I didn't follow in his footsteps and that my differences were what caused his drinking."

"Nonsense. Your father drank because he wanted to drink. He drank to celebrate. He drank if he was upset or sad. He drank because he drank—or as they say now because of a chemical imbalance."

"But isn't it something how he managed to carry on," Ben said.

"Right. He was one of those drunks who could show up at work the next morning no matter what."

Ann thought, "They could be talking about me."

"Let's not talk about him in the past. He's still above ground. A different person alltogether, but quite loveable in new ways," said Kitty.

"That's right," said Ann. "And they may still come up with some way to patch or mend the spinal cord and broken nerves to his brain."

Ben rolled his eyes and made a face. This was always Ann's hope. One the rest of them could not in their wildest dreams imagine.

"Where is Natalie?" Ann asked.

"Gone to bed. Natalie always sleeps a lot when she's pregnant," Ben replied over his shoulder as he walked out to check on the children who were crammed together on the screened porch watching a video. The littlest ones were asleep or almost there. The older ones were staring at the screen, half asleep but trying not to show it. He picked up the youngest and nudged the older ones to follow him to the tent or their beds in the Portable.

"So Helen told me Bernard's not coming over this year. Has anyone got more news?" Ann asked.

After settling the children, Ben climbed the stairs to the apartment over the garage. He looked in at

Natalie fast asleep and noticed the extra hump beside her. Must be Henry, too scared to stay out in the tent with the big boys.

Ben pulled a beer out of the fridge and collapsed on the couch. He thought over the annual meeting. He'd have to talk it over with Natalie tomorrow. He was discouraged that he wasn't able to have a good discussion about winterizing the Portable and buying out the others to make the cottage their full time house. Too many things going on. Too many changes. Too many distractions. Helen, jet lagged and tired, Ann getting drunk, Sarah wanting to sell off the whole place, then rushing to the hospital, Harry and his stupid wedding plans. Jesus, this family is a mess. I'm getting fed up trying to keep things on course here, he thought. And I don't want Natalie to have to put up with all the crap flying around. We need our own house with more room when this baby comes. The Compound is just too much expensive real estate. We could make a killing by selling out. Split the proceeds and go our own way. Nat and I could buy a good house in a nice neighborhood and live happily ever after, if we don't die of boredom first, that's what Natalie would say. She loves all this greater family business, the pulls and pushes of each person on another. While he, himself, wishes they could live their own lives with their own children and not have to be entwined with the family at large.

Bob came to, confused. He couldn't remember why he was in a hospital room. Then it dawned on him and he was relieved to see he was alone. It was wearying to put on a brave face. He wanted time to think. He knew Sarah was cooking up some theory about his being done in by evil forces. Crazy girl. Things were unpleasant in town, but not that bad. What he hadn't told her, though, was about the girl he'd bumped into at Berts who, it turned out, worked for the Hazen Company. She didn't exactly work for them but was a consultant, public relations. Nice girl. They had a drink. She was attractive. He didn't talk about Plymouth and the Hazen project. It was just a chance meeting, he was sure, or almost sure. It was the night of the final game of the Stanley Cup. Everyone in the bar was concentrating on the TV and conversation and drink orders were squeezed in at commercials.

What the hell. Now I can't move my arm. Shit. This is weird. Gotta yell. No can't. Pull the cord. Pull the cord. Sarah walked back into his room with a Styrofoam cup of coffee just in time to see him struggle with the cord. "Help. Help me." She yelled. Rebecca and the doctor rushed in, worked Bob over and got him stabilized.

"Oh my god, Rebecca. What's going on," Sarah pleaded. Rebecca was white as a sheet. "We've got a helicopter just now landing. Mass General emergency infectious diseases unit is ready to take him and take him fast. Frank's been pulling every string he can. I'll feel a lot better when he's there. This hospital is great, but we've got to have the best brains in the business get a reading. Nobody has a good idea of what's going on."

38

Helen woke up at two a.m., eight o'clock Paris time. She tossed and turned for an hour and finally decided to get up. She tiptoed down the hall, trying to avoid the creaking boards, then stepped down the narrow wooden stairs skipping the squeaking one third from the bottom. She made herself a cup of tea and took it to the porch. Might as well grab this chance for a little peace and quiet while the sun rises, she thought. On previous visits she would have sat back in comfort to let the salty breezes wash over her. She would have emptied her mind of all cares and plans and let body, soul and mind absorb the healing atmosphere of this spot she'd worshiped at all her life. Everything was comfortable and familiar, or had been up to this year.

Did it start with Paul's accident? her disintegrating marriage?, Sarah's fear of the power plant?, Harry and Peter getting married? All this within the space of ten months or less. There was an uncomfortable feeling in the Compound. The magic was gone. Undercurrents were destabilizing things. Well, she thought, I'd better tend my own garden first. What should I do about Bernard? Should I try to make myself into a sophisticated French woman and be above it all and seek other outlets? Or should I give him hell, leave him, divorce him, push an ultimatum. A French woman would keep the lid on and, though going her own way, would not divorce for the sake of the family. But how do I react to that plan. It's just not the same for me. I was brought up to believe in till death do us part, with a good dollop of Hollywood happily ever after while walking into the sunset thrown in. I'm hurt. That's what I am.

Five

Ann woke up when Frank came into their room. "What's up? What time is it?"

"It's about three in the morning. Helen is downstairs beginning her day on the porch. They have sent Bob up to MGH by helicopter. He's pretty sick."

"Really? What's the problem?"

"That's just it. We don't know. But he's a very sick man.

"Oh my god." Ann sat up too quickly. "My head is killing me."

" You're drinking too much."

"What do you mean drinking? I may have had a few with the sibs and cousins last night to celebrate our getting together. You don't need to accuse me of drinking in general terms. Well. Never mind. What's the story with Bob? Do you have any idea what it's all about?'

"Nope. They'll run some tests and figure it out. He is in the best place he could be. Let's go to sleep for what's left of the night."

40

Kitty put a pound of bacon strips in the biggest iron frying pan. Nobody in the family worried about cholesterol. Bacon and ice cream were daily fare. The family's medical histories tended to diseases of the head: alcoholism, and various mental disturbances. The physical parts moved along into old age with very little attention and usually led to a long senility period before death. So bacon and eggs, pancakes, waffles with maple syrup, toast and butter, were breakfasts of choice. Granola and yoghurt were for others. Kitty pulled her wrapper around her ample belly and watched the dog through the window, digging up one of his treasures buried in the herb garden. The cat was spooking around, stopping now and then to preen herself in the patch of sun enlarging though the cedars. Parker's car was gone. She had heard them drive in very early in the morning. He must be going for an early visit with Paul. No sign of Priscilla. They needed a good sit down and chat, though this was never easy with her sister-in-law, who was always on her guard. Some night this week she would get that girl out by herself and see if they could let down their hair together. She smiled at the thought. Priscilla's hair was always neat and well cut, nothing to "let down". Kitty used to envy it and the way Priscilla looked. Now she wasn't so sure. Though god knows she brought up her children well. Helen, Ben and Sarah all seemed to be well adjusted, contributing members of society. Of course, this state of affairs might not last forever. There were signs of un-raveling. Helen was quiet and somewhat forlorn looking. Bernard was not coming this year. Is there a rift, she wondered. Ben and his Natalie were terrific, holding the compound together, but there is something a-foot. The rest of them find him a bit distant. Is he becoming too involved with big developers in town? Or is that just his sister talking. Well, anyway, as she turned the bacon, she thought, those kids, not kids any more, seem to be on track, headed toward a life she understood. But her own kids were more complex. Ann had everything, an attractive house in Sudbury, marriage to a successful doctor, three great children. But she was drinking. The old family disease was rearing up in the most unlikely places.

She never told anyone that after Paul's accident among the other things they had to treat was withdrawal. The doctors couldn't figure it out at first. It was obvious that there was severe spinal cord and brain damage, right from the beginning. But what was later diagnosed as delirium tremors, was not immediately obvious. She knew he drank regularly and too much. But he was the sophisticated type of drunk who never made a fool of himself and who got up every morning and went to work. He was (is!! she reminded herself) a good husband, a good provider, a good father. Well, he was quiet and shy around the children. That was his style. I wonder, really, what he'd say about Harry and Peter getting married. She covered it well last night, she thought, telling Harry they always knew and were proud. But she had to admit it was probably a blessing for all involved that

Paul was in another world and wouldn't have to deal with a situation which was beyond anything he could relate to.

The grandchildren began showing up in the kitchen. Strips of bacon were disappearing from the counter before making it to the plate. She scrambled a dozen eggs, put the juice and coffee out, assigned toaster duty to the kids and crossed over to the guest house to talk to Priscilla.

Parker and Priscilla had arrived in the compound at about six that morning. They had driven down from Ontario to Exeter for his reunion and stayed with friends nearby. They left early in the morning to avoid traffic through Boston and arrived in Plymouth shortly after Helen woke up and Frank returned from the hospital. Thinking everyone must still be in bed, they settled into the guest house and took a short morning nap.

Priscilla is a good-looking, self contained woman. After Parker retired they sold their Dedham house and moved to the cottage in the Gatineau, north of Ottawa, for the "season" – summer, fall and spring. In the winter they went to Mexico and rented a house in Oaxaca. Priscilla painted, or studied and talked about painting, Paul sat in the sun and read books, all the books he had always wanted to read when he was too busy, reveling in the fact that at last there were no pressures, no things he ought to be doing. Priscilla had her arty friends both in Canada and Mexico. She was a great supporter of the art scene in both countries and relieved to no longer have to kow-tow and fit in with the Lloyd family or the Boston crowd. She found Bostonians, in spite of their old world reputation, too cynical. Their quick patter and joking insults, although lovingly tossed, were hard to take. She didn't get it. She was straightforward, not one to kid around. She had pretty well broken Parker of these habits. Early in their marriage, when he swore and insulted everyone including her and she would be shocked or dissolve in tears, he tried to explain: "I only insult the ones I love you stupid ass." She was not amused. She did not fit in and she knew it. She raised the children and "did the right thing" while Parker practiced law, became a successful lawyer and then a judge. She was at his side in the photographs, in a nice little suit, with coiffed hair and a loving smile.

But there was not a lot of fun and games in the Parker Lloyd house in Dedham. The household ran well, was well appointed, neat and clean. Summer in the Compound was what their children lived for. Helen, Ben and Sarah could throw off constraints, let loose and run wild. Many summer nights they ended up at the cousins' houses.

The cottage in Ontario was close enough to town for concerts and plays and to see friends and far enough out so that Parker could buy up contiguous land to make his gardens and experiment with self sufficiency, trying to live off the land. That was his caper. Priscilla left him to it while she pursued her career as an artist. They would spend a couple of weeks or less each year at the Compound seeing their children and grandchildren and what was left of Parker's siblings. As it turned out, only Kitty and Paul, such as he was. John was entirely out of the picture, having sold off his share and moving to California.

Six

Parker stopped in for the obligatory visit to his brother at Brewster House on his way downtown to get the paper. It wasn't easy. Paul had that shit-eating grin on his face. Just sitting there in a nursing home, smiling aimlessly day after day. Parker did not sit down for the visit. He stood so that no one would think he was going to stay and it would appear that his life was so busy he just didn't have the time, yet that he was good enough to stop in and see his brother.

"Hello, old boy. How's it going? You're looking well."

Paul smiled. Then he said umph, yeah, umph. A nurse went by and he reached out to catch her and he giggled.

Jesus, Parker thought. What an imbecile. Too bad the damn tree didn't do the whole job. Kill him quickly. What was the sense of this?

"Hey, Parker." Greg Barlow ran the nursing home. He was the only reason half the "loved ones" came to visit. Greg was a sailor, and a supporter of the arts in

Plymouth. His family had been in town for generations. Curiously enough, he was doing just what he liked and he was good at it. He loved and respected the patients/clients and they all loved him (if they were still with it enough to have any emotions). The staff respected him and were happy at their work. And the families enjoyed visiting. Brewster House turned out to be a meeting venue for Plymouth families. Those who could afford it hoped to spend their last days in its plant and art filled corridors and be pushed in their wheelchairs through the award winning gardens. Greg usually had some interesting small talk – a joke or two, always in good taste and applicable to the family.

"How are things going Parker? When did you get in? Spending time in the old Compound?"

"Yeah. Just went to my fiftieth at Exeter. We'll stay a week or so, then I have to get back to the blueberries."

"I hear you had a little excitement last night in the Compound. Bob collapsed?"

"Really? We got in early this morning so I haven't spoken with anybody. What happened?"

"I don't know. There are some rogue viruses roaming around town. Ticks are worse than ever this year. There's a cluster of Lyme disease out on Ellis Road. The whole Williams family has been hit, and that makes it almost an epidemic. And then of course there is the swine flu."

"Well, I don't know much about it. Canada must be too cold for those bloody bugs. We have plenty of others to contend with. How's my brother doing?"

"He is what you see. No changes. He's nice to have around. It's good for morale to have his sunny smile. And I think it's a help for Kitty and the kids. The smile may not mean that he's happy, but it gives the impression that he is. And that's really what the family, any family, wants more than anything. The smile attracts people and there is a lot of joy round him. We're glad he's here. As you can see, not everyone here looks that happy. It's not easy when you're confused and muddled." Greg began pushing Paul's wheelchair down the hall. "So Paul, do you want to take your brother out and show him the roses? Here, Parker, just go out this door and do a tour of the garden walk before you have to go." Greg knew that many men found the visits hard. He had ways to allow them to make them short and sweet.

Parker pushed the wheel chair through the double doors to the garden. "So Paul, here we are. Nice day for it. Kitty's looking well. She loves her role as Grandmother in Charge of the Compound. I know the younger ones, our kids, would happily take over, but they know old Kit needs a distraction." Parker found himself babbling away to his brother. "You're a lucky man having Kitty. She's a lot of fun, and hasn't changed much through the years. There were times when I envied the crap out of you, you know. Yes, Priscilla was a good catch and all that, but Jesus, she is uptight. The problem is she lacks a sense of humor. I finally figured that out. Of course, we can't all be masters of the one-liners and raunchburgers like you and me." He pushed the wheel chair past the gazebo.

48

"Why in God's name, did you have to go and get yourself pummeled like this? Were you boozing it? Cutting trees down at your age was not brilliant, you know." Parker made a few tours pushing the wheel chair around the circular path. "Well, I've got to get back to the Compound. I gather there's a lot of controversy swirling around. Some of the kids want to get rid of the place, you know. I seem to remember Mum, in her theatrical way, telling us she'd come down and haunt us if we ever sold out. Well, it's just not the same. Among other things, the town's all screwed up. Traffic's horrendous, police can't keep up with the break-ins and fights. And there is the chronic looming fear of the nuclear plant. Oh, well, I won't bother you with all of this. Glad to get it off my chest though. Thanks for listening. Goodbye old man. I'll check in tomorrow, if I can make it."

Paul smiled.

Seven

Priscilla was going through her folder of Mexican paintings and drawings. She had taken a course last winter in Oaxaca from one of Toldedo's students. She pulled out a colorful painting: fantastic, surreal, avant guard. No one will get it, she thought . . . I don't myself. But it was fun to paint. Her instructor was better than any shrink. He told her to just let fly. Color outside the lines. Don't try to make any sense out of it, or out of life. Just let your soul take over. See what happens. Don't think, just paint. It worked when she was there. She always felt great in Mexico. But she just couldn't bring it back north with her. Once she got north of the border, especially in the Boston area, especially with this family, her insides began to contract. She couldn't relax. She would spend hours choosing her clothes each day, working on her hair and her face, neatening her suitcase, the bureau drawers, her desk. It never seemed so bad when she was in Canada. There was an order to things in Ontario. And in Mexico, the happy disorder did not bother

her. But you never knew what to expect with these New Englanders. On the outside they look the same as Canadians, they talk almost the same, they dress the same. But there's a difference. She doesn't fit in, never has and she knows it and regrets it. Now at least it's only a few weeks a year in the Compound visiting the family. Each person she likes, but when they all get together she's an outsider, distant even from her own children. They have a casual way about them. The surety of people who have an elevated place in society but don't care, or pretend they don't care. They dress in any old ragged thing, shop at second hand stores, brag about their finds. The less spent the better. It seemed to work well on them, these pre-worn Brooks Brothers shirts and Talbots shorts and blouses. They looked turned out and put together in well worn clothes their hair pulled back with head bands and barrettes, the men with two day growth of beard, the women not caring about their expanding waistlines and thinning hair.

Kitty you-hooed at the kitchen door. Priscilla slid her painting back into the folder and stood up to kiss her sister-in-law. "Hello my dear. How are you? I was just getting ready to go across and see you . . ."

"I'm fine. How about you? When did you get in?"

"Very early this morning. We were tired so we just slipped in here and took an early morning nap. Thanks for making the beds and filling the fridge."

"Not at all. I'm so glad you're here. I guess Parker's gone down to see Paul?"

"Yes. He wanted to get it over . . . oh, I didn't mean that ..."

"That's OK. It's hard on him, I know. Men don't take well to that sort of thing. Not that any of us do. But somehow I think we women are able to cope better."

"Oh Kitty. It must be hard on you."

"Actually, I've about settled into it. It's just a way of life now. It's been almost nine months, you know. I'm not expecting miracles (though some of the kids are) and in some strange way, actually, I enjoy my gentle visits with Paul. I read or chat. He smiles. You know, if he looked angry or upset or frustrated, it would be harder. But, though it may not mean anything, he appears peaceful and content. I've no idea what's going on in his head, or if anything is, but I've decided to just accept what I see. As it turns out we had discussed things and made living wills just before it happened. I've told them down there if anything changes we want no extraordinary measures, as they put it. I told Greg we don't even want flu or pneumonia shots. Although he's stable and comfortable, he wouldn't want to live on like this forever. These nursing homes can be sort of cocoons, protecting the old folks, in ways the rest of the populace isn't from accidents and disasters, which could well do the rest of us in. Meanwhile, nursing homes protect the halt and the lame, the senile and the . . . Oops. I didn't mean to jabber on so long. Tell me about you. Have you seen the kids?

"No. Helen came over early apparently; she left a note. I wasn't up. She took the kids to the beach and will come back for lunch with me. Ben is at work. Natalie and their kids went to the beach with Helen. I don't know where Sarah is. I thought she planned to be here for the weekend.

"She went up to Boston. I guess you haven't heard. Bob had some kind of attack last night. Collapsed in the outside shower. Frank is really worried, which means it's serious. He's been on the phone with doctors at Mass General."

"Well that's awful. I like Bob a lot. And of course so does Sarah."

What a cool cat, thought Kitty. She didn't say anything.

"What's the matter?" Priscilla asked.

"Well, it's just that I'm awfully worried. I guess since I've put aside the worries about Paul, I'm now concentrating on the whole brood, the generation under us. Your kids and mine. They are like one big family to me. I think I've adopted yours to think about during my tossing and turning nights and they're right up there in the hierarchy of loved ones. Right on the same level as mine. I guess it's because you don't live here all year."

"No, Kitty. Face it. What you really think is that I've opted out. Not just from living here, but from all my responsibilities. As far as I'm concerned, the kids are grown, they have their own lives. They make their own decisions, do their own thing. And the best thing I can give them is their independence and let them make their own mistakes.

"I guess you're right. But I find this compound living so healthy. We're like a small village here. The family can hold together and support each other. The grandchildren are free to run from house to house and have more than just play dates. I don't know how it is in Canada, or in your part of Ontario, but most children have no freedom, no relief from the parents and the parents no relief from the children. Nuclear families live in houses with fences around them. Children are whisked off in SUVs to sleep-overs where they watch videos all night.

Kitty was called the grandmother in charge of the compound. Her sister-in-law didn't get it. Priscilla couldn't understand why she held on to her grown children nor why she fiercely held on to the real estate: The Compound. Let them go she wanted to yell. Give them their lives. Don't cling to the past.

But Kitty loved this spot and the multi-generational family who gathered in the summers. She had grown up on a farm in southern New Hampshire. The farm included a few cows, a flock of sheep, chickens, pigs, a vegetable garden. Maple syrup was the cash crop. She remembered mud-filled early spring days helping her father collect sap to bring to the evaporator for boiling down. The smell of it, mixed with the smell of his sweat. She helped her mother make maple sugar candy by boiling the syrup longer, to the soft ball stage, and pouring it into maple leaf and sea shell molds her mother had designed. She and her brother were constantly busy, always working, pruning, feeding, weeding, gathering, making, canning, selling. Her family worked. Work was their god.

But then at age fifteen she pulled away from her family. She started running around with the alluring, tough and terrible crowd in Manchester. Her mother, fully occupied with the candy kitchen and part time teaching at the local community college was distracted and gave her a long leash. They were a close family, but not a family to show affection. No hugs, no kisses, no I love you. They were old Yankee and didn't like to broadcast their emotions.

Kitty took off one night with her boyfriend of the moment. She got on the back of his Harley and drove north to Canon Mountain just for fun. They stayed out all night. The next day driving home, holding on to the leather jacketed waist of the boyfriend loving the freedom of feeling the wind in her hair she worked on inventing the story she would make up to tell her parents. Some unlikely tale they would believe.

They roared in to her town at about eleven and drove down the road to the farm. Police cars and fire trucks lined the road. She thought oh no, they've called in the police to search for me. And then she saw it. The house had burned to the ground. Where were the parents? What had happened?

Her brother survived, but was in the hospital for months with burns. The rest were gone: her mother, father, the dog, two cats and the house and all that was in it. Kitty ended up in a mental hospital for almost a year. With good therapy she was brought out of the guilt and depression. She moved in with an aunt, worked hard at school, got accepted at Wellesley and met Paul. One of the things — no, the thing — she loved most about Paul was the Compound. The give and take of a large family interacting if only for a few weeks each summer.

It's just that I think we have a special place here, Priscilla, and I hate to see it break apart."

"Is it breaking up? I didn't know."

"Something is going on. The kids, yours and mine, had their so called annual meeting last night. There's some controversy about whether or not to hold on to the Compound."

"Why don't the ones who don't want to keep it sell out their portions to the ones who do?"

You cold blooded bitch, Kitty thought. She said, "It's not an easy thing to accomplish. The ones who want to hang on may not have the funds to buy out the others."

"What's the deal? Who wants what? Wait a minute. Do you want some coffee?"

"Thanks. I'd love some." Kitty sat back and looked out across the water at the lighthouse. She thought about her first time at the Compound. It was Labor Day 1955. Paul invited the whole gang for the weekend. Although they were not going out, Paul and Kitty were part of the same circle of friends. That weekend they began to fall in love. She had just finished school and was going on to Wellesley the next week; he was starting his third year at Harvard. It was not love at first sight, but it began to develop. And now, fifty years later, she was looking at the rocky beach where they first began to flirt. Back in those days, they got to the beach by rickety wooden stairs over the cliff. They all clamored down, about ten of them, and sat on the rocks and swam, drank beer, made jokes and ate sandwiches. Paul and the boys swam out as far as they could, racing and seeing how long they could stay in the water. The ocean was colder then. Now it's not so cold as to turn your legs numb and send you out with hypothermia if you try to swim more than a few minutes. They could thank the nuclear power plant for this. The ocean water sucked in to cool off the turbines, was sent back into the ocean hot. The lobsters and swimmers loved it. The environmentalists warned against upsetting nature's balance. But back in 1955 it was cold and the boys joked about how it shriveled their manhood.

That weekend in Plymouth led to fifty more years off and on of dragging gear down the stairs through the gulley on to the rocky beach: picnics, towels, snorkels and masks, fishing rods, canoes, kayaks and paddles. Paellas. Also grandchildren, friends, relatives, ancient aunts, French visitors, Dutch and Canadians, too, sunhats, umbrellas. They made forts in the rocks of the sea wall—the boys did—the girls made houses and hotels. They skipped stones, swam to the boats. Grandchildren are now behaving as they did, and as their children did. The power plant just isn't enough of a threat to give all this up, she thought. And where in the world is safe anyway?

"Where are the coffee filters I wonder," Priscilla was rifling through the cabinets.

"Oh, I don't know. We're probably out. Just use paper towels."

Priscilla hesitated, then thought what the hell. She said, "Now tell me what our mutual children are cooking up."

"Here's how it breaks down, starting with your children Helen would like to keep things exactly as they are forever. The Compound is her get-away and relief from French life. Ben and Natalie want to move from their apartment downtown to something bigger because of the baby. They'd like to winterize the Portable and make it their own. Sarah's the one agitating for a complete sell-out. She is convinced the power plant is unsafe. She thinks it might blow up or be attacked by terrorists and that there's leakage now. You know how people can always find clusters of cancer when they look for it."

"You certainly have your fingers on the pulse of what my kids think . . . and I don't mean to sound jealous or teed off. I'm very grateful they have you. You are the mother figure to the whole bunch and we're all lucky you are."

Kitty said, "I didn't mean to fall into this role. I guess it just happened because of events beyond my control. And yet, I do feel strongly about this place. The history and the soul of this piece of land. It's almost a sacred place for the family. Think of the things that have taken place here."

"That's just it," said Priscilla. "For me it conjures up things I'd rather forget. And, what's more, I feel in some ways this place is like an albatross hanging around our necks. Holding us back, draining us both financially and mentally. But now tell me about your two. How do they come down on it?"

"Ann feels the way Helen does. She wants to hang on and keep things the way they are. I'm not sure Frank is crazy about compound living. I think he'd prefer to have his evenings and weekends to himself. It doesn't help being a doctor. He's always called on for advice and cleaning up wounds and removing splinters. But he goes along because Ann and the children are so attached. As for Harry, he too wants the compound to stay as it is because he wants to keep it as a home leave address, not only as a place to stay, but a place to vote from when he's abroad. By the way, he told us last night he's getting married."

"That's interesting. I thought he was a confirmed bachelor."

"You mean you thought he was gay. Well it turns out he's marrying Peter."

"You must be kidding."

"I'm not. Apparently they're planning a big wedding here in September."

"Oh lord."

"I know what you're thinking. But we're all accepting it and I've never seen Harry so happy. I told him that Paul knew he was gay before the accident and it was not a problem."

"Is that true?"

"It may be stretching the truth a bit, but that's not going to hurt anyone. I hope you'll come for the wedding. It would mean a lot to Harry."

"Of course we will," Priscilla said, though she wondered whether Parker would go along.

"What our children are eventually going to have to face is the legal and financial burdens they will take on once our generation bows out. I think Parker, you and I should sit down this week and figure out how we're going to pass this along. I don't know how Parker and Paul worked it out when John sold out. I guess it was an even split. But now, with your three children and our two and all of them pushing for different needs and configurations and having different financial situations . . . it's not easy."

By the time Frank woke, Ann was up, showered and on her third cup of coffee. The kids had wandered down to the beach with their cousins and she could see them out the window fooling around on the kayaks and canoes. She listened to Frank's progress overhead through the single layer of planks making up the floor above and the ceiling below. He clomped down the hall in bare feet, took a pee, did not flush (as instructed by conservation notes posted in the bathroom) threw water over his face, clomped back to the bedroom pulled at a stuck bureau drawer, swore, kicked the bureau, yelled goddammit, pulled and shook the drawer. Finally he descended the creaking wooden stairs and appeared in the kitchen. Ann couldn't help grinning through her headache.

"Gimme some coffee, damn you. I know you heard it all. My yearly first communion with the damn Big House."

"I thought you were remarkably restrained. Especially on just three hours of sleep."

"I'm looking forward to getting out on the boat. That vision kept me from losing it all together." His cell phone rang. "I don't like the sound of the ring."

"Frank. It's Patel at MGH. We've got your boy stabilized but I still don't know what it is. We've put his blood through every test we have and it's not Lyme or Denge or any of the possible insect born infections. Not viral or bacterial. It almost looks as if he got into some poison. We're going to do more checking of stomach and intestine contents."

Frank knitted his brow and replied, "I have no idea what I can add to this. If Bob's sister is still there, you might suggest she check with the family and see if there's any odd poison around the house or shed that might have gone astray. Thanks for all you're doing Patel. You're the expert and we are all very grateful for your help."

"Not at all. I must say it fascinates me. I've never seen anything like it."

"You think he'll pull through?"

"He's going to need a lot of care for at least a month. I don't know."

"I'll talk with his family about follow-up. Any idea how long you'll keep him?"

"His sister is pushing to have him sent back to Plymouth. I don't see any reason not to have him put into a nursing or rehab facility but I'd like him nearby for a while to I can keep an eye on him."

"OK. I'll talk with you tomorrow."

"What's up? How is Bob?" Ann asked when he put down the phone.

"They don't know for sure. He's in good hands. I'm going fishing."

Eight

Stuck, stuck, stuck in this stupid body. Can't move, can't speak. They think I can't hear and can't think. Well, I've got them fooled there. My damn brain is working fine, probably better than ever now that it doesn't have other things to do such as telling my hand to hold a fork, telling my foot to take a step, or telling my face to frown. Apparently all I do is smile. As Parker calls it, my shit-eating grin. Everyone thinks I'm happy and content. Well, OK. If that gives them pleasure, let them think it. I probably won't hang on much longer in this earthly coil, in this body out-of-control. They deserve a little happiness if that's what they're getting out of me after what I've put them through.

Ah. Here comes the team. Clattering down the hall, with my wheelchair, whispering away. Now at the door. They don't know I see them. They think I'm non compos mentis. "Hi Paul," the pretty young one yells. They think I might hear if they yell loud enough. I like her. I try to say hello, but all that comes out is an extended vowel. G Sharp whole note.

The battleaxe says a polite, "Good morning Paul. Time for us to get dressed. We have a busy day today." I tell her to get lost. It comes out D flat to B flat slur.

"I'll get your clothes out Mr. Lloyd. Khakis and blue shirt today." That's Victor, my male nurse. A pansy, of course, but that doesn't bother me. He's damn good and the only one, including the family, who believes that there's something going on in here, inside this lousy wrecked body of mine. Victor talks to me man to man. He never talks like the others do, over or around me, as if I don't exist.

Of course it's not all bad being in this condition. I can snoop and listen to conversations not intended for my ears. I can think my thoughts, review my life and remember my favorite poems. Thank god I was forced to memorize at school. And if I have left any legacy at all at Lisburn, I did get them to adopt the routine of having the boys memorize one poem or sonnet or something each week. I said to the head when I made this suggestion you never know when you might want to dredge up some words of wisdom. You might be stranded on a lonely island, perhaps, or taken prisoner in Turkey, or stuck in Amsterdam without your luggage. It's then when you can select Henry IV's soliloquy out of your deep memory file, bring it up and reflect on it at your leisure, on its meaning; or Yeats. Get these boys to memorize, I said. It's only by memorizing that they will fully get it. And it may save them from insanity some day. Little did I know at the time that it would be me who would get the greatest benefit. I memorized from an early age. Nursery rhymes, Milne, the Gettysburg Address, Bible verses, psalms, Shakespeare, Frost, Yeats. Somewhat controversial was my plan at Lisburn Academy. Lisburn, like the other old New England schools was getting more liberal. Getting away from anything that smelled of rote learning, stupidly having kids play with cuisinary rods rather than learn their times tables, sloughing into letting the boys supposedly pick up knowledge, letting them take easy sciences such as oceanography and star gazing instead of giving them chemistry and physics. No Latin, no Greek, no classics. I brought the old three R's back when I was headmaster, but I brought on a lot of pissed off parents, especially the old grads whose kids couldn't take the heat.

Oops here I go, they're lifting me now. Changing my diaper, pulling on my clothes. I'm putty in their hands. Don't feel a thing, but there are sensations. Thank god the battleaxe has left. I reach out to give the pretty young one a pat and got her left breast. My right arm and down the side has some movement. It always surprises them when I catch them unawares. But that's what a pretty girl will do to an old man.

"Visitors today, Mr. Lloyd," Victor says as he lathers up my left cheek. "Your wife is coming with the children and Parker's children as well. They're all gathering at the compound for the Fourth. It's a full house, or full houses, I hear."

Oh great. They'll all be standing around me discussing my state of decrepitude and my funeral. Tell them to mind their own business, I said to Victor. Which came out D, F Sharp, D in half notes slurred, a drone.

"I know it's not easy. But they won't stay long. I'll tell them you're tired or something," Victor said as he finished up my shave.

Sarah rushed in just after they had set themselves up in the corner of the large common room at Brewster House. Victor had delivered Paul in his wheel chair and told Kitty that Paul was tired and might not last for more than a half hour before needing to stretch out on his bed. Kitty said fine, they had time only for a short visit. She kissed Paul on the cheek. "Well, sweetie, we're all here. It's been a while since we've had the whole brood under one roof. Everyone wanted to see you, so I thought we'd all come together this time."

"Hi Uncle Paul," Sarah gave him a quick peck on the cheek. "Sorry I'm late. Just came in from Boston. Bob's really sick. I think he was poisoned."

"Sarah for god's sake. Don't go there." Ann said. "Dad doesn't have any idea what you're talking about. Even if he did, we shouldn't upset him about stuff like that."

"Yeah, and besides it's just your own paranoid conjecture," added Ben.

"What are you talking about Sarah? What makes you think he was poisoned? Who'd poison a nice guy like Bob?" asked Helen.

"You have no idea what's going on in this town. There are national corporations wheeling and dealing, making deals with the power plant, buying off town hall. There are big developers who want to put in huge houses on the land next to the power plant. The buffer land, the land with beautiful views of the ocean and all the way to Boston. Bob's looking into it and . . ."

"All right. Enough. We're here to visit Paul and the kindest thing we can do for him is to keep the conversation positive and upbeat," said Kitty. "Imagine what it's like for him. We don't need to air our dirty laundry here."

"What are you talking about Mum? Dirty laundry? Dad's probably bored to death if he is taking anything in at all, which must be what you think. If so, let's give him something to chew on and think about during the dreadful endless hours. Let's see what his reaction is if we talk about selling the Compound."

"Come on Harry. You know that's not an issue," Ann said.

"Oh yeah? Well we sure got an earful from Sarah about it at our annual meeting before Bob got sick. Before she rushed off to see lover boy, Sarah said that we should get out while the getting is good."

"We are NOT considering selling the compound," said Kitty. "Now let's change the subject."

"Why change the subject? You've put the place in our hands. We need to take charge."

"Oh come on Ben. Give us a break. This doesn't need to be discussed here. Call another meeting."

"Well, I think the parents, all four, ought to be in on it," Helen suggested. "We don't want to go behind their backs."

"Yeah, Mum," Ann added. "We know you always want everything to be nice and all of us happy. But you have to realize. Things have changed a lot."

"OK, said Kitty. What is going on. How do you all think about the Compound being sold?"

"I don't, think we should sell," said Helen. "It's my only American home. I want our kids to at least have one foot in this country and not be totally French."

"I'm the same way," said Harry. "I need an R & R home when we're on overseas assignments. And even from Washington. I wish we could leave off talk like this until after the wedding. There's enough else to plan for this summer."

"Oh for god's sake Harry. You're not really going ahead with a stupid gay wedding are you? Why do you have to make such a big deal of this?"

"What do you mean by that? It's no big deal. It's a Massachusetts law. You had a big wedding. Why can't I?"

"That's enough. Let's talk to Paul and not squabble. Paul, I see Brewster House is preparing a float again for the parade."

Paul smiled and groaned.

"What do you think, Ann? Frank's not crazy about compound living, is he?"

"He says not. But he loves getting off in his boat. I don't know where else he can do that, or where we could ever buy another place close to Boston. The children have completely signed on to compound life. I agree with Mum. The Compound becomes more and more precious as life in the big world outside becomes more and more complicated. Our children are lucky to have this place where they can run free from house to house, to beach and back. I'm getting more like Mum. I would declare at the beginning of each summer a moratorium on televisions, computers, telephones, blackberries and the like. Maybe I'd just turn off the electricity and throw out the batteries. Let the kids run around in shorts and tee shirts. Let them get bored, lie under a tree or climb it, build a raft, make forts . . ."

"OK. That all sounds lovely," said Sarah. "But don't forget there's an aging power plant just around the point ready to exude noxious gases and beckoning to terrorists."

"Come on Sarah. There's danger everywhere. We have to keep living."

"The thing we have to work at now is the finances of the place. The parents have put it in our hands. I think what we may need is an outsider, a money manager consultant who can look over the whole picture with us and work out a plan. Maybe it will turn out that some of us want to sell out. We need to see the finances of this. To see whether those that want to stay can afford to buy out those who don't."

"Sounds to me as if it's only Sarah who wants out. Who sees danger in staying."

Sarah started crying. "It's not that I don't love the Compound. It's just that I read stuff. And now with Bob poisoned."

"Wait a minute. We don't know that he was purposely poisoned. Something may have gotten into his food was the way Frank described it, according to the hospital."

"Still, I'm very upset about it and about the latest NRC reports on the power plant."

Nine

Helen was the first to leave. She stood in the nursing home parking lot waiting for the rest of the family. She hadn't seen Paul since the accident. The others had. She was shocked, numb. She felt sure he was taking everything in – that he was trapped inside a body he couldn't function. What did he think about? What were the rest of them thinking, carrying on in front of him over and around him as if he didn't exist? Kitty pretended he could hear. She yelled at him nice wifely things. The rest of them made their usual wise-guy jokes. Ha ha, devil may care, cover up all feelings, talk about the weather, talk about the traffic, argue about the Compound. What about how you feel? Helen was hurting. She was raw. When the rest of them trickled outside and were working out who would go in which car, she pulled Ann aside and suggested they stop downtown for a drink. Ann quickly agreed, as Helen knew she would.

"Bloody Mary," Ann told the waiter.

"Coffee for me, please."

The restaurant was empty; it was before the lunch crowd. A lousy little restaurant, really, in downtown Plymouth, but it was a favorite. It was gloomy and dark, with a thin strand of light coming in between awnings. Shabby booths lined the walls. There were a few tables in the middle and a bar along the back, beside the door to the kitchen, with a neon sign flashing Budweiser. The Hungry Pilgrim for fifty years has served what is now called comfort food, such as meatloaf, mashed potatoes, and string beans out of a can. It is probably the only place on the east coast where you can order any one of three colors of jello for dessert. On Thursdays they offered liver and onions. The place was usually packed.

"I wanted to talk with you alone for a while, Ann. I am very sorry about your father. It must be hard."

"Oh we're getting used to it now. But thanks. What about you? You seem, I don't know, a little distracted this year."

"Bernard is having an affair, the bastard," Helen blurted.

"I somehow thought that might be the case. How long has it been going on? How are you coping?"

"It's been a few months since I found out. So the pain of the initial blow is now somewhat lessened. As you said about your father – it takes getting used to. But I'll tell you something. The heart really does break. That's not just an expression. I felt a pain, a crack, right in the heart area. It kept me awake for almost a week. The pain turned to sadness, anger, fury. I was so alone. Of course it is part of the French culture – taking a mistress at a certain age. But I had figured Bernard would be different since he'd been to school here. Not that I really thought about it that much before it happened."

"How'd you find out?"

"Marie Claire, my friend, his partner's wife, told me. Though I think I was aware before she told me. It's his secretary he's screwing. She calls herself his assistant."

"Yeah. Some assistant. What did you do?"

"I haven't done anything yet. I'm being French about it. Keep the family together. Take a lover . . ."

"No! Really? Do you have a lover?"

"No. But I'd like him to think I do. Or I should say them to think I do – his family and friends. The worst thing to be, in French eyes, is a long suffering, martyr type of wife. I agree and will not have people pity me."

"Good for you. I think I'd kill the shit head. Or at least make his life miserable."

"Well, maybe. Actually I've thought about it a lot. Not of killing him but of what I want in the end. And what I really want is to rise above it somehow. He'll get over her, but there will be others. Yet his sense of family is strong. I'm pretty sure he'll get back to me fully at some point. So the trick is to figure out what kind of a person I want to be. The worst moment was when she walked into the restaurant in June. It was New York month at Le Brunch. I was serving Oysters Rockefeller, bagels, cream cheese and lox. It is a lot of work but the French love it. We played recordings of jazz, *New York, New York, West Side Story*. Things were going well and I was chatting to one of the young waiters when I spied her out of the corner of my eye. Damn. By then I knew about the affair, of course, but I just didn't know what I was going to do about it. God knows I'd spent enough sleepless nights thinking about it, crying, or furious. But I didn't let on. I didn't say anything to Bernard. I wanted to be prepared when I confronted him with it. I needed to figure out whether to leave him or what to say to him. So I put it on hold. Anyway, I was so busy at Le Brunch I had no time for myself. But when that bitch walked in, struts in on her big heels and short skirt, slender, young, stylish, I didn't know what to say to her or not say to her. I thought I'd have more time. I went into the kitchen to stay out of her sight. I had to toast some bagels anyway and get the salmon on platters with mounds of cream cheese. The bar was set up and full. No wine. That is my rule. I don't want the French to be looking down their noses at American wine so we have wine only during San Francisco month – Napa Valley. That day, in honor of New York month, the bar was serving martinis and manhattans. It goes over well, these regional American months I'd set up. The French are fascinated to find that American food consists of more than McDonalds and Coca Cola. The Texas month had been a great hit with Tex Mex, margueritas and beer during the Super Bowl game. Oh yes, it was all a marvelous distraction for me. I was so wound up and excited about my little project that I totally mislaid the fact that Bernard was not paying much attention to me anymore, and that, according to Marie Claire, he had taken up with his secretary, his assistant as she called herself, the little bitch."

"God. This is interesting. You're amazing to have gotten through it so well. Now you have some time on your own to think it through." Ann called the waiter. "Another Bloody Mary. How about joining me for one Helen?"

"No thanks. I find I can't drink much of anything until evening. In fact this is something else I want to talk to you about. I'm thinking of opening a Le Brunch branch here and wonder if you would go in with me. Be my partner."

"Oh. Wow. That sounds great. But I'd need to think it over. Yes, of course, I'd love to . . . but I don't know. I'm pretty busy. Tied up with things I'm not sure I can get out of . . ."

"Ann. You know you can do it. I'm going to be straight forward and direct like the French. You have a big problem and it is booze. It's about time you faced it. You've got the old family disease that snakes through our mutual family and pops up in the most unexpected places."

"Oh shut up, Helen. You act as if you know everything. Why don't you mind your own business? You know nothing about what I have to put up with. Dad comatose, with an idiot smile on his face, but possibly not brain dead, just stuck in an unmovable body. Mum trying to hold things together. Harry marrying Peter. Frank works till seven or eight every night then comes home needing peace and quiet and the full spread: drinks, a good dinner with wine, brandy. Me stuck in suburbia, chauffeuring the kids around all day. What do you know about all that crap? You living in high and mighty elegance in gay Paree."

"OK. Ann. All I'm saying is you drink. You're an alcoholic like most of the rest of the family. And the sooner you admit it the better your life will be. You probably didn't know that my father is a member of AA. He keeps it quiet. And certainly your father drank, though he was a functioning drunk. According to Ben, he was drunk when the tree fell on him at noontime. And who knows about Uncle John. Has anyone heard from him? So considering those three brothers, our fathers and uncles, there's a pretty strong genetic argument for your addiction."

"You're just noticing it now cause I'm celebrating being with you."

"You drink to celebrate. You drink to drown your troubles. You're not fooling anyone."

"Why don't you shut up?"

"Because you're my cousin and my best friend and I hope you will come into business with me. But I'm not sharing my business with a fall on her face drunk."

They sat for a while simmering, saying nothing. Two angry women in their mid forties in a bar in downtown Plymouth on a Saturday morning."

Finally, Ann said, "Truce. Tell me what you have in mind for Le Brunch."

"It's been incredibly successful in Paris. As I said last night, who would have thought?! The French feel Brunch is so American, so droll. It's become something of a "see and be seen" place for the in crowd – the tout Paris. I wish you had gotten over this year to visit and see it in action."

"What is the secret? What do you serve?"

"We do the usual brunch things such as eggs Benedict and Florentine, bloody Marys and Mimosas. We have couches and comfortable chairs around and various sized tables. It's supposed to be like home. On weekends we do regional buffets: Boston, New York, San Francisco, Dallas and New Orleans – one or the other for a month. Small combos play jazz or folk music or we play CD's with music to suggest the region. It's pretty ersatz, but the French eat it up, literally and figuratively."

"Give me an example of a regional brunch.'

"OK. I told you about New York month. And Texas. I jettisoned cod fish and baked beans for Boston this year, and served Thanksgiving instead, a simple Thanksgiving with sliced turkey, mashed potatoes, squash and cranberry sauce. We always serve cranberry juice, by the way. The French admire it's tartness and its healthful qualities. I worked a deal with Ocean Spray and they ship me bottles for practically nothing. I've convinced them that it's good advertising. Sometimes our food is a challenge for the French. I'd say what is most baffling for them though, the most foreign, is the buffet, the help yourself aspect of it and sitting on couches or standing while you eat with only a fork. They are used to being served and eating at a table with knife and fork."

"Fascinating. But what about here? If you set up a le Brunch in Boston, what will be the theme, the trick to get people in the door?"

"That's what I need you for. To put our heads together and think of what would work. Since it's called le Brunch, maybe we tip the idea over and turn it into a French idea of brunch. Serve café au lait in bowls."

Ann added, "Potage, onion soup, croissants, an accordion player."

"Yeah. See? We can go wild with ideas. Money, thank god, is not a problem. Le Brunch Paris is doing well and Bernard has wanted to expand, though I don't think he had in mind expansion across the ocean."

"It may be a good time for him to consider it."

"Exactly. In fact I've been playing with the idea of living here for a year. The children are at a good age to do a school year abroad, to experience life in America."

"Oh, I see," said Ann. There's a method in your madness. You would have a year here to distract you from marital problems and for Bernard to see what he's missing."

"That's sort of what I'm thinking – and I wouldn't have to confront him or make scenes."

"It makes sense."

"Thank you for hearing me out and for your input. I could do this on my own, I suppose, but I really would like to do it with you. Of course I'm hoping after a year to go back to France."

"As I said. I'll have to think about it. There are a lot of pressures right now."

"Screw pressures. Take a leap. Remember how we used to play Truth, Dare, Consequences and think up the hardest dares. Well this will be a hard one for both of us."

Ten

Sarah sat on the guest house deck staring out to sea. She was exhausted and let her mother wait on her. She brought a plate of salad with bread.

"I'm glad at least you have Frank to help you through this terrible time," Priscilla said to her as she put the plate on the table. "I gather he's keeping in close touch with the doctors at MGH."

"Yes, Mother. It helps, but this is very scary. They can't figure out what's wrong with him. They've done every test they can think of for virus and bacterial infections. I think he was poisoned, but no one wants to go there."

"Poisoned? What on earth do you mean?"

"There is a lot of money at stake here. Hazan Corporation is trying to develop the extra land around the power plant and Bob has tried to stop it. In fact, I want to ask Daddy about Hazan. Didn't he own stock in the company?"

Priscilla sat down at the table. "You really shouldn't get stressed about this, Sarah. You're tired and fantasizing about wild possibilities. You've always had an active imagination, but this is over the top. You read too many mysteries."

"Oh never mind, Mother. Stay removed from everything as you always do." Sarah got up from the table, plunked herself down on the hammock and pulled a towel over her face. "Just leave me alone. I'm going to take a nap."

Oh damn, thought Priscilla. Things were not off to a good start.

Helen and Ann walked across the lawn and up the deck steps. "What's going on? Where is everyone?" Ann asked.

"Frank's out in his boat – he asked me to tell you Ann. Ben is at work and Natalie has taken various kids down to the beach, as you can hear. Sarah is over there, under the towel."

"So that's who it is. I'm sure she's exhausted. She got very little sleep last night." Priscilla, Helen and Ann chatted quietly about the weather, the children. None of them were comfortable to talk about what was really on their minds: Helen's separation, Ann's drinking, Priscilla's problems with Sarah. They skirted their real emotions. They were used to that.

"Telephone for Dad" Lizzie yelled out the screen door.

Her grandmother, in the garden weeding, said, "I think he's out on the boat. Run across to the guest house and ask your mother."

"Mum," Lizzie yelled, "It's the hospital calling Dad"

"He's not here. He's out sailing. Wait a sec. Tell them to hold on. I'll be right over to take it."

Ann walked across to the Big House and took Frank's cell phone, the only phone in the Compound. All other phones had been banned this year as part of Kitty's experiment in anti-progress summer living. "Hello, this is Dr. Moran's wife. He's not here right now. Would you like to leave a message with me?"

"It's Dr. Patel at Mass General, Mrs. Moran. About his patient, Bob Meyers. Is there any way I can reach your husband?"

"No. He's not here. He should be back in about an hour. Can he call you then?"

There was a pause on the other end. "Please have him call me the moment he comes in. He has my cell phone number or he can call the hospital directly and have them page me." Dr. Patel hung the phone up before Ann could reply.

Ann is not usually aware of Frank's work. They live in separate orbits. She has not seen him in an emergency like this. He comes home tired late in the evening. She's usually exhausted herself and slightly tipsy. She always has a glass of Merlot at about five to get her through the evening routine with the kids, reminding them to do their homework, get off the computer or phone or ipad. She'd have another wine while she cooked and fed them. They were always fighting about something. Though by the time Frank got home, the arguments would be over and the children on their way to bed. He would say a quick goodnight to each one while she cleaned up their mess, re-set the table with candles, and opened a new bottle of wine. He wouldn't notice how much she had drunk, as long as all was in order for him at the table. Nice day, dear? Oh fine. She'd tell a few amusing anecdotes about the neighbors or the children and ask how things were at the hospital. As usual, he'd say. Things are going well. Had a Saudi prince today who needs a transplant, may work it in for next week, etc. She would have another glass, stack the dishes, turn in early to be up with the kids by six to get them off to school. Frank would grab a coffee to drink on the commute. But watching him deal with Bob's emergency and to see his kindness and compassion with Sarah was to see a whole new side of her husband. She wondered if he missed the one on one patient care. He seems hardly to have the chance to be with people now that he is a famous surgeon at Mass General. His patients were prepped and ready for him to operate, while they slept. I'm going to ask him, she thought. I'll cut back on the wine . . . find a way to be close again. I'll chat with Helen and consider the Le Brunch plan. We could move into town, out of the suburbs. Set up a restaurant here in Plymouth or in Boston, live over the store, or closer to the hospital for Frank. I wouldn't drink so much if I weren't stuck in the suburbs. Do I dare take such a big step? If Helen is going to, maybe it is the right time for me. Maybe we all need a change.

    She wrote a note for Frank to call Dr. Patel and walked out to the vegetable garden with notebook and pencil to confer with Kitty about menus and the shopping list. Tradition dictated hot dogs and hamburgers, potato salad and watermelon on the night of the third and poached salmon, peas and new potatoes for a late lunch after the parade on the Fourth. A pot luck picnic takes place on the beach July Fourth night around a bonfire, while watching fireworks across the bay.

Kitty, squatting between the rows of peas, looked up at her daughter, "For the first time in years, we have enough peas in the garden for the Fourth. I've ordered the salmon. You can pick it up for me down at the fish market. Check with Helen about the cookout and picnic supplies. As you know, I only do the lunch on the Fourth and give over the other meals to the rest of you. Parker and Priscilla told me they'd take care of drinks, Ben and Natalie are doing desserts and watermelon. But wait, I said I'd stay out of the planning.

"Thanks Mum. You're right, no reason we can't organize the rest."

"What did the hospital want?"

"It was Dr. Patel. He wanted to speak to Frank. No message. I told him Frank would call him when he got home. I left him a note."

"I hope everything is all right," Kitty worried.

"We'll know more when Frank gets back."

Later, Frank found Sarah in the hammock at the Guest House. ""Sarah are you awake? He peered under the towel. I just spoke with Dr. Patel. Bob may be ready to leave the hospital next week. Dr. Patel suggests that he is ready to move to a rehabilitation place, but would like him close to the hospital. Could you coordinate with his family. I'll bow out of this case now."

"Thank you, Frank, for all you've done. So what did Dr. Patel say? What happened?"

"He's not at all sure. He thinks Bob was run down and therefore more susceptible whatever it is that hit his system."

"They don't think it was poison?"

"They just don't know."

Eleven

"Stop moping around, Ben. We can make do. This apartment is cozy and we can expand by turning the garage/pigpen downstairs into another room. Let's give the summer a few more weeks to shake out. Bob's seizure, or whatever it was, threw Sarah for a loop. All of us, for that matter. And I think Kitty is more upset than she lets on about Paul. It can't be easy for her. It's only been nine months since the accident. Let's make another stab at a family meeting and see how people feel about us buying out the Portable for ourselves. If it doesn't fly, we can rent a house somewhere in town and keep the Compound as a summer retreat for the family. That is, unless they vote to sell the whole property."

"Natalie. I love you! You are wise and understanding. Of course you're right. No hurry on this. Give me some credit though. I was thinking of you. Isn't there a nesting instinct that happens to pregnant women? I figured you'd want everything set before the baby."

"We've got the servants quarters here and the apartment downtown. That's fine with me for now."

"I hear Helen is thinking of opening a Le Brunch over here on this side of the pond."

"Yes, she told me on the beach today."

"Is she leaving Bernard?"

"No I think the plan is to move over for a year."

"No trouble in the marriage?"

"I don't know. Maybe so. But I think she may just want to be around the family here for a while and give the kids a taste of the culture she grew up in."

Sarah's theory that Bob was being poisoned was in the back of everyone's mind and a subject they skirted in conversation. Was it absurd? Was it possible? The rest of the people on Boards at Town Hall apparently were enchanted by the Hazen Company. Small town potentates loved rubbing shoulders with and being wined and dined by slick, well dressed wheeler dealers from New York.

Priscilla asked Parker about the Hazen Company. Did he think they were capable of some sort of plan to remove Bob and get him out of their way?

Parker looked closely at his wife for the first time in years. Priscilla had given up the weekly visits to the spa and the hairdresser. Some might say she had let herself go. Her skin was pale and covered with fine lines, like parchment paper that had been crumpled into a ball and then spread across her fine bone structure. Her hair, for many years twisted into an elegant French knot, expensively colored ash blond, was now unabashedly gray. She wore it tied back with a ribbon. What had once been a slender well dressed woman on the arm of her husband, the judge, a woman who had worn becoming fitted suits with pearls at her neck, a woman who seemed cold, frigid, without humor or compassion, was now a seventy year old artist who wore loose clothes, no makeup and seemed more approachable. Parker replied that he had divested his stock in Hazen Company years earlier. He hadn't liked their bookkeeping practices and felt the company was too cozy with government agencies, and lobbyists. He told her he would talk to Sarah about it later that day.

Parker joined Sarah on the beach that afternoon. With snorkels and masks they swam through seaweed and poked through the rocks looking for crabs and lobsters. Afterward they arranged themselves on the hot dry rocks to rest and dry off. "Look, Sarah," he said. "I know you are nervous about the power plant and that you think the family should sell the compound and move away."

"I don't want it, Dad. I just think we have to. Pilgrim is exactly the age and model of Fukushima. And though we are hardly likely to be struck by a tsunami here, there are other possibilities including terrorist attacks and human error as well as natural disasters such as hurricanes, tornadoes and earthquakes. That plant is just too old and too unsecure."

"I can understand your concern and hope you, your siblings and cousins will come to an amicable agreement about the Compound. Your mother and

I trust you all completely. I also wanted to talk to you about the Hazen Company. I did own stock and got to know some of the principals. But I sold out and cut off any relationship with the company five or so years ago. I didn't find them trustworthy. Now, whether they're capable of doing someone in, of poisoning Bob, is a serious accusation. I will call a few people and do a little research on the company and see what I can find out."

For the most part the family glided along through summer. Although there were nagging issues that needed to be addressed and decisions that needed to be made, they were left unsaid and eventually seemed to dissipate as the daily activities of summer in the Compound took precedence. Fishing, lobstering, meals, gardens, marketing. There were traditions to uphold such as birthdays, anniversaries, reunions; there were races to run, contests, games, art projects. There just wasn't time or inclination to worry about the power plant or the future of the Compound. And Kitty continued to insist that the worries and cares of life outside the Compound be left at the end of the driveway so that everyone would enjoy the pleasures of warm summer days.

This is a test.
This is only a test.
The emergency warning system will be testing for the next 10 minutes.
This is only a test.

The speaker on the tall pole across the road from the Compound blared out the message from the nuclear power plant. A flock of alarmed starlings rose as one from their perches on a nearby cedar tree. The human population paid little attention and like other annoyances managed to fold these announcements into the rhythm and noises of daily life. Children played on the beach while jet skis buzzed across the bay like angry insects. Cell phone towers on the peninsula across the bay had sprouted like weeds. The lighthouse was no longer the sole sight on the horizon. It had been replaced with psychedelic green lights, flashing a steady warning. The entrance to the harbor now resembled a landing strip at Logan Airport. The deep bass voice of the foghorn had changed to a computer driven high whine which often misfired and continued its racket even on bright sunny days. How did this happen in the course of a decade? The power plant reminded people with computer voice on their phones at the beginning of each month, via reverse 911, to turn the pages to the next month in the handsome calendars they provided at the beginning of each year, calendars with brown and white sepia photos of the good old days in Plymouth. They suggested that at the same time each family member glance again at the evacuation routes and the suggestions on how to prepare for emergencies. The calendars provided a wealth of information on things to have on hand, food and medications places in the house to ride out an emergency. Schools were provided with a hefty supply of medicine to counter the effects of radiation.

People joked about it at dinner parties. They scoffed at the idea that anything could be done, should something happen at the plant, a leak, an explosion, a terror attack. They were sure there wouldn't be any way to drive away from the radiation in time, evacuation route or not. Should it happen during school hours, parents would certainly not leave town without their children, as instructed, but would head straight for the school. In any case the roads would be clogged – there were so many new housing developments close to the plant. Plans were laughingly made with friends to meet in someone's basement with a good supply of gin, books and playing cards.

The plant tried to quell concerns. The "outreach" department invited the Board of Selectmen and other elected and appointed town officials to tour the plant. And they invited the League of Women Voters, the Chamber of Commerce, Rotary, even anti-nuke groups for a tour. They held symposia and informational forums at Town Hall and the Library, which was broadcast on the local TV station that nobody watched. Meanwhile, one sturdy anti-nuke stalwart of a certain age, sailed her cat boat right up to the shore in front of the plant. She told the world she had done so in a newspaper interview which got national attention. Headlines:

"70 year old Plymouth Mass. woman claims she could have loaded her sailboat with explosives and blown up the power plant."

Meanwhile supporters of the plant pointed to the grimy yellow line of smog along the horizon on certain days—the outfall of a coal fired energy plant about fifteen miles down the coast. Is more of this what you want instead, they'd ask. And how about the recent coal mine disasters in West Virginia, China and Chili? And importing oil puts the country under the control of the whims of the often unstable oil rich countries. We are already at war in the middle east, and jittery about our other trading partners. Isn't nuclear power a better way than fossil fuels, they would argue. Windmills have been rejected up and down the east coast as too intrusive, ugly, or a hazard to migrating birds. We have no choices.

The Lloyds would read the articles, and be urged by one side or the other to contact their congressmen. The anti nuke people asked them to sign petitions insisting that certain things be improved at the plant before any new contracts were made between the town and the power plant company. That a safe environment be constructed for the spent rods and that a better evacuation plan be devised. Some older citizens were blasé about all of it. They tended to see the plant as just one more of many possible dangers one must face in life. Those who had lived through wars, floods, hurricanes, forest fires could not bring themselves to worry overly about this particular potential disaster. They saw disasters as part of life.

Their children, the thirty to fifty year olds were the ones most consumed with safety. Have a Healthy and Safe New Year was the message on their Christmas cards. Merry and Happy were out of fashion, pushed aside by healthy and safe. Accidents, disasters, diseases, even death, could be avoided with sufficient vigilance. Seat belts and helmets were called for, sturdy SUV's that would not crush on impact were encouraged. Fire alarms and burglar alarms were installed. They enthusiastically lighted up dangerous, dark nights. Regular checkups were made of their bodies, X-rays, MRIs mammograms, colonoscopies, camera probes were sent down the throat to meet those going up the rear end, blood pressure readings were taken, and electrocardiograms. Some wore gizmos to keep a daily check on heart beat, blood pressure and sugar levels. They had flu shots, took pills to lower cholesterol, relieve arthritis, rejuvenate the blood and thicken the bones. Women took hormones, and then men took Viagra to satisfy their wives' new hormonal induced sex drive. Dogs were fixed and children were driven to play dates, potholes were filled, roads widened. Smoking was abandoned as was the eating of red meat. Defibrillators were installed at parks, schools and playing fields. There were hand sanitizers inside the doors of most public buildings and bowls of condoms in some. This age group wanted to be sure the nuclear plant was absolutely safe. Yet they had little time to do anything about the nuclear plant; they did not show up at meetings or demonstrations or go door to door collecting signatures.

The Lloyds loved the memories of their compound. They loved remembering the times before constant vigilance and modern communication changed life so radically. The general thinking, if they thought about it all before this summer, was that in their compound, on the two acre chunk of land with three shacks, they could live life as it used to be – the way they remembered it as children and the way it was lived by earlier generations. They tried to keep the place simple and cling to the old ways. They planted hedges and trees to absorb traffic noises and hoped that by squinting at the gorgeous ocean view, they could blank out the cell towers and neon lights on the land across the bay. They tried to ignore the possibility of nuclear power plant seepage, explosion or melt down. Of course they could sell off the Compound and split the rather large proceeds. But then what would they have? If indeed the power plant was a real and present danger was there another place they could go, either as a family or in separate nuclear (perish the word) families, that would be better, that would not in some way develop other dangers or annoyances?

Twelve

Finally, Ben called a family meeting to finish discussions that had been interrupted by Bob's emergency in early July. They met after supper in the dining room at the Big House. Ben had spoken separately with each person before the gathering hoping to find points they would agree on. Here it was August and they were still not certain of what to do. The spouses, Natalie and Frank, sat in on the discussions but did not insert their opinions.

"This is what it boils down to," Ben got everyone's attention after dessert. "Is the Compound worth holding on to? We have to start there before we move on. Has the threat of the nuclear power plant got you scared, or is the price of repairs and up-keep of the houses too much? Should we sell out and leave?" He was agitated. They could see that. He was at war with himself, not sure if he wanted to sell or to stay. But one thing he did know was that he needed a decision. The rest of them sat around the table listening to his tirade.

"Damn it," Sarah broke in. "You're all blaming me for even bringing it up. I don't want to leave. But living next to the power plant is dangerous. Even if we ignore fears of terrorist attacks, or breakdown of the reactors, the spent fuel rods are not secure. The power company did not build anything for long term storage. The rods were supposed to go to Yucca Flats. Three thousand rods are now stored here in a space meant for eight hundred.

Helen sat in an uncomfortable ladder back chair looking down at her plate, thinking about the year to come, about leaving Bernard and her Paris life about setting up the new restaurant with Ann, renting a house, settling the kids into school. She was dead against selling. She needed this spot. She needed it as a get-away, for the short term and for long term as well, whether or not her marriage could hold together. She looked around as the others squabbled. The Big House dining room held a hundred years of rejected wedding presents in corner cupboards and on shelves: bowls, teapots, demitasse cups. The hinged windows, pulled to the ceiling were held up with hook and eye. The spatter painted floor hid spots of spilled food and crumbs; there were two quarter sized holes drilled through the wood so that on particularly messy nights, when lobster juices and corn butter was dribbled and drinks overflowed, the room could be washed down and the water drain out through the holes to the ground below.

Cigarette buts were stubbed out and floating in the mass of melted vanilla ice cream on Ben's dessert plate. Ann helped herself to red wine, the cheap Chianti they always drank. Her face was showing the ravages of drink, her eyes half closed, and her skin flushed and coarse. She spoke with a slur. Sarah was wan and tired. Still insisting that Bob had been poisoned, she had taken it upon herself to get someone to investigate the possibility. She spent every spare minute hounding the police and town manager. She was frazzled. Her pretty naïveté had been lost in the constant struggle. She played with her spoon, twisting it through her fingers, the nails bitten to the nub. She maintained that the power plant was a target for terrorists, that before long, perhaps on the upcoming tenth anniversary of nine eleven it would be the next great conflagration.

"So," Ben said, after much discussion. "How do you want to handle this? Shall we take a vote? Or do you want to discuss further? Natalie and I really need some kind of decision here. Do we sell or do we not? Or, do we decide not to decide? That too would at least be a decision." He lit another cigarette, his hands shaking.

"I say we decide not to decide." Harry said. "I just want to have my wedding and get on with my life. There's no reason to believe that the plant will explode or whatever tomorrow."

"Tell us about the wedding plans," Ann said. And the table conversation moved on to chatting about the guest list, flowers, photographers.

Kitty, Parker and Priscilla had retired to the living room after dessert before the meeting began in the dining room. Parker was splayed out in the large arm chair, its springs scraping the floor. "What other choice is there? Nuclear is our best possibility. We have to stop our dependence on oil. Look at the problems with oil, the wars in the Middle East and spills in the Gulf of Mexico. We need energy and lots of it. What other choice is there if not nuclear power? It is clean and certainly better than coal fired plants."

"Wait right there," said Kitty. "I'll tell you a choice. Turn off the lights. Put on a sweater".

"Oh come on, Kitty, don't be naïve."

"Naïve?! Why does there have to be so much consumption? We're not actually using the so called necessary power to produce a damn thing in this country. As far as I can see it's used only to light up the night sky and keep ourselves too hot in the winter and too cold in the summer. We should live more naturally. I don't mean we should go way back to primitive times, only that we should be more aware."

Priscilla spoke up, "I have quite a few friends in Ontario who have installed geo thermal energy in their houses. Office buildings in Toronto are doing the same. And, listen to this, there was an article in the newspaper with photos showing clothes lines running through the rooms of certain of the grand old houses in Toronto with wash drying. It was in the Art section. People are vying with each other to make the most artistic displays of drying wash in their living rooms and front halls."

They were quiet for a few minutes. Pretty hard to top that one. The Canadians always seemed one step ahead on matters of reason, goodness and civilized living.

Parker said, "Did you know that Ben is almost set to copyright his little gizmo that turns stationary bicycles, treadmills, and rowing machines into power sources for heat and light? Apparently people love watching the arrows showing how much wattage they put out for every minute they exercise."

"I didn't know that," said Priscilla. "Good old Ben. How's he coming along on uses of spent rods? I thought that was his major work."

"I think he's still working on it," Kitty replied. "That would be such a break through."

"Well, Ben's the guy to do it. I would say one of Plymouth's greatest accomplishments in recent years was to set him and other bright young people up in that 'Incubator' think-tank in the old factory in North Plymouth, where they can come up with solutions for present day problems, including global warming and renewable energy. With great minds such as his there may be some hope on the horizon. Small things like getting energy from exercise machines, sounds silly but at least it gets people thinking and moving along to find solutions to bigger problems."

"Another idea for the nuke plant," Kitty added, "is to make use of the boiling water to heat greenhouses after it has cooled the reactors before it is sent out into the ocean. Somebody ought to consider setting up greenhouses on the land near the plant. We could have locally grown fruits, flowers and vegetables all year long. Speaking of flowers and vegetables, have you ever seen such a bountiful year? I've never had such plump cucumbers."

"I'm anxious to get home to my blueberries," Parker said. "They'll be at their peak by next week."

"What's the best route to get through Boston?" Priscilla asked. "We're off at the crack of dawn."

They continued talking in the gathering dusk, moving seamlessly from subject to subject, while barely hearing the background noises of arguments and laughter from the younger generation in the dining room.

Parker and Priscilla pulled up just outside Burlington at a squalid looking motel. Parker was still reeling from the visit. Priscilla was now the stronger one. She had felt more a part of his disparate and difficult family on this visit. She had at last accepted the fact that though she did not fit in, though she had for more than forty years felt slow and dull witted and not one of them, she finally felt worthy in a different way. She was comfortable in her own skin. Years of yoga had made Priscilla calm with a zen approach to daily life. Parker opened the trunk and pulled out their overnight bag. He was tired. The changes rolling across the world were more than he could fathom. The Japanese tsunami was bad enough in its own right. But it also brought into the family's personal life threats and fears and an undercurrent of instability. His face was gray and wrinkled. Brown spots stood out on his balding head. What was left of his hair was dull mousey brown. The jaunty bow tie, penny loafers, khakis and blue checked shirt showed to those who cared that he must have gone to one of the ivies. But this type of dressing, he thought now, was not fitting the new gloomy atmosphere of today's world. Nuclear waste, the spreading of toxic material through the water and air was a danger none of the wars he had lived through or the wars he'd read about had equaled. He was confused and uncomfortable with electronic gadgets, the cell phone, ipad, tom-tom and kindle. He had given up taking photos because he simply felt too dumb with his old fashion camera. He was angry and dispirited by anything that smacked of political correctness. He had always felt he was fair and without prejudice, but recently he seemed to come up against hard and annoying arguments about diversity, feminism, racial and sexual changes. There was no zest for life left in him. Parker was troubled by the sight of his brother, stuck – maybe not even brain dead – in a body he could not move. He was also troubled to see his children consider selling the compound, the family safe-haven from the gloom and terror of the world outside.

"Come on Parker. Cheer up. There's nothing you can do about things. What happens, happens. Let's have a drink in the room then go downtown for dinner. We have to get up early to make it home before dark."

Helen had written to Bernard in mid July and told him she was planning to stay in Plymouth and would spend a year in the U.S. He wrote back a very rational, elegant letter respecting her decision. But Helen could read between the lines. He asked why she hadn't written to him before making this decision. He made a joke of it, saying she was trafficking his children across national borders; he mentioned kidnapping. She had told him in her letter that she wanted to be nearer her family, especially Kitty, who was dealing with Paul's vegetative state. After all, Kitty and Paul are really like parents to her, she had pointed out. As he knows she is closer to her Aunt Kitty than to her own mother, and Kitty is more comfortable with her than with her own children. She had written to Bernard earlier that she had bumped into an old friend who wanted to open up a Le Brunch in the area. To be her partner. He asked about that in his return letter. Who is this man and what is she getting into and how are his children going to manage in a new school while she's off philandering plus setting up a business? It was slow going having these discussions and arguments by mail. They were keeping in touch like Abigail and John Adams, not in the way communication happens in 2011. But since phones, computers and all their variations had been banned from the compound, this was the way they "talked". In some ways it was easier, and it was certainly more civilized. Their conversations might have been reduced to shouting matches if they had picked up a phone.

Many things were left out in their correspondence, swept under the carpet. She and Bernard never discussed his mistress. She knew that he knew that she knew, but neither wanted to bring it up. She let him believe the lie that the old friend, her partner to be, was a man. She didn't tell him it was Ann— well it would be Ann if she could get off the sauce. Bernard gave the impression that he couldn't understand how anything would be better than her returning to be with him. He liked having her around when she was the good natured old girl who kept his house and family in order while at the same time running a popular and successful restaurant. He loved having all that and the joys of a pretty young mistress on the side. He didn't know that Helen had changed. She had lost weight (which is what a broken heart will do, she thought). She planned to get her hair cut and buy new clothes. She would set up an office in the factory where Ben had his, the so-called Incubator, where start up businesses and researchers could have space rent free for a year. She would work out of there until she found the right spot for Le Brunch. She'd stay in Plymouth and find an old house to rent downtown; put the kids in the local school. It might not be as great as living near Boston, but it could work. She would not stay in the Compound in the winter. She'd rather keep it as a summer retreat, an island of peace and harmony remote from the cares of the world. As far as her feelings about the nuke plant, she was never very concerned. France for years had been a great believer in nuclear power. There were plants throughout the country, there was an ambiance of acceptance.

Helen drove to Brewster House and found Paul in the garden. "Let's move into the shade," she suggested pushing his wheel chair to the gazebo. "You're looking well, Uncle Paul. What shall we talk about?" She chattered nervously about picnics and fishing expeditions, the family and the Compound. Gradually she began talking about herself. She told him how hard she was finding it to decide where her allegiances were. Whether she was more French or American. She told him she didn't feel part of either culture. "Even in the Compound I'm not comfortable and don't fit in. I've been out of the country too long. It worked while Bernard and I were new and in love. I counted on him. We were happy straddling both cultures. What a fool I was. I should have studied French culture better before throwing myself into life with him. If I leave him, could I ever be settled here?"

Paul grunted melodious responses, which Helen understood as encouragement to continue her line of conversation.

"I'll talk with Ann again and tell her what I'm going through. We're planning to open a restaurant together—an American Le Brunch. But I told her I couldn't do it with her until she stops boozing. She thinks I have it together and that I dismiss her, which isn't the way it is at all. We're both a couple of closet addicts. She drinks, I eat. A fat woman waddling around Paris is less than nothing. I know it is one reason Bernard has taken a mistress. Sure, I'm comfortable and fun and a rarity and everyone thinks I'm fine and jolly with it. But that is far from how I feel."

Paul smiled. Helen continued her monologue. "Don't you think we've got to hang onto the Compound? It's a precious hunk of land, in a dysfunctional town, in a messed up country in a scary world. We have to cling to it and to each other. If people can make themselves whole and make each family work, maybe we can fix the world. By raising our children to be leaders they might be able to pull civilization out of the mess we've gotten the world into. I'd like our kids to understand simplicity, to listen to Aunt Kitty, to use less and have more time to research and study; to live beautiful lives and set examples to others. That may be the only way to go. The French have figured out how to live the day to day life. They live la vie quotidienne, their daily life made simple and beautiful by ignoring stuff they don't need or don't need to know about. In that way they live in beauty with less."

She stopped as if to hear his reply. "Well, enough of this. Thank you dear Uncle Paul for listening. It helps a lot."

Thirteen

Back in my nest at last. Victor has me laid out flat on my back. This is how I'll lie in my coffin. I'm getting plenty of practice. Christ. What a world we live in. I wouldn't be unhappy to check out sooner rather than later. The family is in a quandary about the Compound. They're all over the place, the kids, bless them. I love them all. I get a big kick out of hearing all their worries. God damn it though, I wish I could join in. Well . . . then again, not really. Even if I could put in my two cents, I'm better off just listening. Kitty ought to do the same. It's time for our generation to step aside. Let them work it out among themselves what the hell they want to do with the Compound. Sarah's got a point after all. The power plant is a worry and the Compound is damn close to it. The place wouldn't have a chance if something happened at the plant (nor would we if we were in residence). But, on the other hand, God knows something could happen anywhere in this old world.

Speaking of you, God, do I have any chance that You would pay some attention to the likes of me now? I know I've been anything but a model citizen and I have a lot of *forgiveness asking to do. Are you listening God? Can I get a little help here from You? I really don't want to linger on here. I accept and believe that it's up to You and You may have plans I don't know about. But I find it hard to imagine that You would want me to hang out here much longer in this place soaking up funds and earthly resources that could be put to better use. I'm asking God. Please consider letting me die. Come on. Give me a sign or something. Do You want prayer book words? I could pull up some from my memory box, old lapsed Episcopalian that I am . . . I believe in God, the father almighty, maker of heaven and earth and in Jesus Christ his only begotten son . . . I could go on if you would like and it would help. . . . I'm going nuts here. Oh great. Here comes the medicine trolley. I don't want medicines. Don't they know that? Didn't Kitty tell them. I know I heard Kitty tell them – she better have. We made a deal Kitty and I . . . Well, I'm going to pretend to swallow and then spit the damn pills out if I can.*

"Here we go Paul. Time to have your pills. Just two little pills for you to take now I've cut them in half to make it easier for us to swallow."

Frank's cell phone rang. It was for Kitty. "Kitty, it's Greg down at Brewster House. The nurses are having problems with Paul. No, it's not that he's flirting with them. He's refusing his medicine and he spits his food in their faces. I'm not going to beat around the bush with you, Kitty, or choose my words carefully. We know each other too well for that. We have two options. Force feed him or put him into the hospice wing. I know some of the family feel a spinal cord repair discovery is just around the corner and want Paul to hang in. And some of you want to let him go. I'm sorry this decision has to be put into your hands." He paused and continued in a sad low voice. "At one time, not so long ago, doctors and medical facilities would quietly make such decisions. But that's no longer possible and medical innovations can keep us going forever." He paused again. "Well, you know all this. I won't dwell on it. Let me know, though, if you'd like to get together with Evelyn Santos, the social worker. She might be able to help you make some decision."

"Thanks Greg. We should have given clearer instructions earlier. It's hard, though. Some of the kids feel that Paul is alert in there and that he's telling us to keep him going. Can we wait till after the weekend. I'll be ready to talk about it on Monday."

"Sure. I understand. We'll gently encourage him to keep eating and we can slip the medicine into his food."

Did you hear that, God?! That god damn Greg. He knows damn well I can hear him. Very clever. OK you asshole. I'll be a good boy till Monday. D, F sharp D.

Kitty called Parker and Priscilla. Priscilla answered and asked how things were going. They went through the usual phone conversation preliminaries. "How was your trip home? What's the weather like there?"

"Greg called this morning." Kitty said. "Paul's spitting out his food and won't take his medications.

He told me we have the choice of tying him down and force feeding him or putting him into hospice."

"Really? I didn't think Paul had the ability, physically, to make decisions."

Suddenly Priscilla was silent. Kitty said nothing. They had been hit with a new realization. Paul was telling them something. "I'm sorry," Priscilla said finally. "I didn't mean. . . ."

"No. You have just said something really interesting; two things really. One is that Paul is aware and two is that Paul wants out. This has got to be my decision. Harry and Ann don't want to let him go. They think a cure, solution, or whatever you call it is going to be discovered and that Paul should hang on and wait. But he's seventy-one years old for heaven sake. And we did make living wills and promised each other we wouldn't use extraordinary means to stay alive if we reached a certain point of disability. The thing though, with Paul, is figuring out and deciding when that point is. Well, maybe that's true with everyone. Medicine has come so far and we can be kept alive almost forever. Someone's got to make this decision for Paul. We could discuss it in the family forever. I'm his health care advocate. We're each other's, really. I'm not going to go over this with the kids. In fact they don't even need to hear about it. Oh Priscilla, thank you so much for helping me, for talking with me about this. I am so grateful to you."

"Thanks – but I didn't say anything really. I'm only sorry not to be back in the Compound to be with you during this. Please know that I think you're doing the right thing. Actually, Paul helped you along here."

"I'm going to Brewster House now and sit for a while with Paul and tell him what is happening. I will thank him for giving us his opinion. I also want to make sure that this is what he's asking for. And another thing, Priscilla. I have concluded that you are absolutely right about letting go of the kids and their decisions about the fate of the Compound. Paul had told me before the accident, that I had become too much of a mother hen. You, Parker and I need to get together with a lawyer and have the place put into some kind of trust. I'm sure the kids will be able to duke it out and decide how to divide it up or sell it off or whatever."

"Where's Mum going? asked Ann as she carried bags of groceries from the car into the kitchen of the Big House."

"Down to see your father."

"But we just visited him."

"She wants to be alone with him for a while," Helen replied.

Kitty pushed through the double outside door and galloped down the hall to Greg's office. "All right," she said. "What is going to happen? What I want to know about is what you will do if he keeps pushing away his food and medicine.

It was late afternoon and Greg was just about to leave the nursing home and go for a sail. He said. "Sit down Kitty. Just relax. Let's talk about this. Paul isn't the first person I've seen do this."

"Yes, but we didn't think he had the will, the intelligence, the knowledge to make decisions. Now he's showing he's decided he wants to die."

"Maybe."

"What do you mean 'maybe'? If he won't eat and won't take medicine, he's telling us something. God knows I don't want him to go. Even as he is, a big lump of useless flesh, I still love him. I still like to be with him. I didn't know anything was going on in that battered head of his. I figured he was just hanging out, sitting around in the wheel chair watching the world, such as it is here, go by. Not knowing."

"Well, actually life here may have amused him for a while. But he's been quite agitated since the family visit last month. I suspect he's thinking about things. About life. His life, yours, the family's. Tomorrow will tell. Let's see what happens overnight. This business of refusing to eat may be temporary." Kitty left Greg's office and went to Paul's room.

She walked into the dusky darkened room. There he was, lying like a corpse on his bed close to the window. The roommate's bed was empty, more than empty it was stripped of its sheets. The plastic covered mattress was propped on its side airing. Must have died, she thought, the third roommate to die. Paul's going to get a reputation.

Mocking birds were caroling their evening song, taking turns at the bird bath outside the window. Birdsong almost covered up noise of the trolley clattering down the hall with evening medications. She could hear Wimbledon on a distant TV. Fifteen Love. She couldn't see whether his eyes were open or not. He was smiling – as always. She moved about the room, straightening pictures and mementoes on table top and bureau. Photos of their children and grandchildren and of herself. Framed letters and awards. The old compass for winning a fishing contest when he was eighteen. A marble egg one of the grandchildren brought in. Cards, plants, flowers. On the walls the children had hung collages of photos and she had tacked up a chart of Plymouth harbor. Opposite the bed was a print of Eight Bells, his favorite Homer. All this decoration with the enduring hope that he was aware, could remember. Jasmine was in bloom under the window.

"So old man. I'm on to you now. You're in there and you've known what's going on all this time. Well push over you old lug of an unmovable body. I want to lie down with you one last time and have pillow talk."

Kitty climbed in beside Paul. There wasn't much room, but she managed. He lay on his back smiling as always and gave a happy groan c g sharp e slurred.

"What are you doing? Singing our song?" She lay on her side, snuggled up and put her arm around his inert body. "Well, the way I figured it out— it was Priscilla, really—was that when you spit out the food and knocked aside the pills you made a decision. You see I didn't think you were capable of making a decision. Will you forgive me you old dear? I should have know better, seen the signs. Well, in any case, here we are. You have decided to let go and move on to whatever awaits in the next life. I know you believe there's something. I always loved your idea of heaven as that place where all your friends and family live, a village where everything works and there's no traffic and there is an unlimited supply of Mars bars, rum, and blueberry pie. Well go ahead on. Don't forget we always agreed we'd meet up. Prepare a place for me and don't take up with any of those pretty broads who died young. First though, I'll have to get the funeral organized. I think a little Mozart to start. Oh. I have a great idea. I'll try to get the boys choir from Lisburn. They could give a few rousing bars of the old school song and then some of your favorites; Jerusalem, The Old Rugged Cross."

Paul moaned Agh in B flat moving on to e in a minor mode.

"Oh, all right we won't go there. But I'll find other good old hymns for the gang to sing. They'll want to do something special for you. I could get the new headmaster to speak. No, better to get Eaton or one of the other department heads who can tell some stories. They all loved you so much. You had just the right touch with the boys and with the teachers. They'll never be another one like you at that school. I hear they still quote some of your pithy remarks at morning assembly.

"I'll see if I can get Wade down from Trinity. I would think he'd agree to do the service here for you. Then we'll have the reception afterward at the

Compound. Get a tent. No catering – pot luck will do fine, will do better. Shoot, I wish you could be there. She gave him a squeeze. Well, actually you will be I'm sure. Once you get rid of this useless body you'll be able to float around and visit whenever you like."

Kitty lay there. She was crying softly. It was a relief in a way, but she would miss the old man, her lover her husband, her friend. Even in his vegetative state, he was fun to be with. "Paul, since you are a vegetable, what vegetable are you? Certainly not string beans. Maybe a squash, a large overgrown summer squash, what they call a swede in Europe. I wonder why they call it a swede. Do you suppose it's derogatory? Big fat overgrown swede. No not you. You would be a pumpkin; a nice jolly pumpkin who will be chosen by the cutest kids to take home and be made into a jack o' lantern."

"Let me tell you the gossip from the Compound, old news by now, but a good story and one the kids are still telling. A Canadian family rented the Brown's house. Four boys and their rather bland parents. They looked nice but I never did get over to see them before the international incident. The kids, our kids, had all been collecting firewood for days before the fourth. Little Joe had taken the canoe way down to the point and as he paddled back he stopped along the way and piled driftwood in. Meanwhile the others were collecting stuff nearer by. There was a lot this year after the winter of northeast storms. Jessie pulled a railroad tie over. Sammy worked a telephone pole end over end. This was to be a major bonfire for the Fourth. Well, Priscilla, Parker and I were having dinner in the guest house and I noticed smoke from the beach. It turned out the Canadian bastards had lit the fire – and on July 2, not even on Canada Day, as if that would make a difference. We were outraged. Parker yelled down – 'hey what the hell do you think you're doing?' No apology or anything, in fact the father even looked put out. The next day when our kids saw the once huge pile of wood in ashes they were furious. I tried to calm them – said it was just a cultural difference, that maybe they didn't understand the significance of the collected wood. But our gang was ready to storm the Canadian house, have a fight, stone their car. I said now let's calm down. I was thinking this is the way wars start. I know that if you had been in the Compound. you would have woven it into a wonderful lesson in politics and history. As it turned out the Canadians have made themselves very scarce. I guess they are taking a lot of touristy trips to the Cape and Boston rather than having a holiday by the ocean. Don't you love it though? The ugly Canadians. Such a wonderful change from the usual, from the days when we used to sew maple leafs on our backpacks."

"Well, that's some of the news from the Compound. I'm still being a pain in everyone's neck by insisting that news and communication from outside does not filter into the Compound. It's all bad news as far as I can tell and I see no reason to disturb ourselves with some flood in the middle west or drought in the south, much less a volcano in south America or a tidal wave in Asia, or murders, rapes and other horrors. There's not a damn thing we can do about any of it. But they are agitated, the ruling generation, our children and Parker's, about the nuke plant and the possibilities of another Fukushima – that's the nuke plant in Japan that got knocked around by a tsunami last March. They're talking again about selling the Compound and moving the family to safer ground, or of dispersing and each taking a share of the proceeds. Frankly, I have a feeling they'll never get themselves organized enough to come to any decision. It's driving Ben crazy. He has taken on the chairmanship if you will and is the one in charge of the whole situation, the finances, the assignments. They haven't made much headway since they were all here to visit you over the fourth.

"Meanwhile Bob is in a rehab place in Boston. I suppose you knew he was sick. Sarah's young man, that nice Bob Meyer? He was terribly sick and when Mass General dismissed him they wanted to put him here at Brewster to recover, but then decided it was better to keep him closer to his doctors at Mass General. Sarah is a mess about it. They are such a nice couple. She thinks he was poisoned. He was making a lot of trouble about the nuke plant even before the tsunami. She thinks either someone from the plant wanted to shut him up, or someone from a construction company who wants to build on land near the plant. I think it's a pretty crazy idea, the poisoning.

"It's good to lie here and talk to you again. I've missed you. I will miss you." Kitty dozed off.

"Time for our meds, Paul." The night nurse with the loud voice announced. "Yikes! Who are you!?" she screamed at Kitty.

"I'm his wife. He's not taking pills any more or food. Thank you, but please just leave us alone for a while."

Fourteen

They were sitting on the banking watching the sunset, while the children played a noisy game of capture the flag at the bottom of the lawn. Kitty was in Boston talking with her lawyer and would return on Thursday with Harry and Peter.

"I know Aunt Kitty won't approve of my mentioning it here, but we do have to make a decision about the Compound," Ben said.

"She won't let us talk about worldly things inside the Compound," Ann said, "because she feels, and I agree, that there need to be places people can go to slow down, relax. It's why people travel to remote islands and far away deserted beaches and mountain tops. To find spiritual sustenance . . ."

"Oh come on Ann. Since when did you get all touchy feely and religious on us?" Ben cut in.

"Don't tell me, Ben" said Helen, "that you don't understand. We're bombarded with news of disasters, floods, fires, terrorism, murders, rapes. We need to declare a peace zone. We're lucky we have it here and we should thank Aunt Kitty for her attempts to create such a place for us."

"OK. I'll go along with that," said Ben, "but we can't ignore the behemoth two miles down the coast. We've got to talk about the nuclear plant. And we've got to talk about the Compound and we've got to talk about whether Aunt Kitty's absurd vision of what we ought to be when we're together here fits, in fact, what we can be."

Sarah said, "OK. So we won't talk about it here. We won't contaminate the Compound with negative thoughts and conversations. But let's get together somewhere else. What's happening now among us is an undercurrent of uncertainty and fear and we need to get it out on the table."

Ben suggested meeting in the Board Room at his office, in the factory. "Meet me there tomorrow at five after everyone's left."

They went to the Incubator the next day: Ben, Sarah, Ann and Helen. Harry was in Washington. He wanted to make sure the State Department knew about his up-coming marriage and that his next posting would include Peter on the travel orders. He had told the others that he'd go along with whatever they decided about the fate of the Compound. Of course he hoped they would hang on to it because he and Peter would have a home leave every two years and he would like nothing better than to stay in the Compound. He admitted, though, that he was a minor player and couldn't be much help. However, he would willingly contribute to the yearly minimum upkeep charged to those who did not actually use one of the houses during the summer season.

Ben met the others at the door of the old factory and led them down the hall to the so called Board Room. The group of young engineers, scientists, nerds, intellectuals, weirdos, and inventors, who worked with Ben in the old factory, enjoyed the idea of being in the same place with like-minded types. Mostly, though, they kept to themselves, smiling over their computers as they tried out fantasy ideas and worked on unlikely inventions with the twin pleasures of no interruptions and no rent. The "Board Room" was their little joke, where they had lunch. There was no Board and very little communication of any kind among them. The huge battered table in the middle of the room had been hauled in from the former chairman's office. It was surrounded by a mélange of plastic and folding wooden chairs.

"OK", Ben said. "Let's admit, we haven't been thinking recently about things beyond what's for lunch and what time the tides are right for sailing. We've had the annual meeting in two parts without figuring out what it is we want to do. Now we're closing in on the end of the summer. We need to come to some decisions, not only for the long term, but also for the short term. I'm sorry to intrude on these halcyon days and be the bearer of bad news, but there are bills to pay. I have everything on Excel: the taxes, insurance, electricity and whatever repairs have been done. I've divided your payments by time spent by each of you in the Compound, scaled to which house you've lived in. So here is what each of us owe." He handed out the spread sheet. They looked it over and nodded their agreement and mumbled their thanks to him for taking care of it all. They promised to send him their checks.

"Now for the longer term plans. I'm the outside guy. I still escape the Compound and come to work every day. Though we're an odd ball bunch here at the incubator, mostly up in a cloud and playing with our crazy ideas, we are aware of what's happening out in the big world. The guys who come down from Boston and from other places outside Plymouth are amazed that we appear to have our heads in the sand. They don't understand how we seem to ignore the nuclear plant. Especially after Fukushima."

Ben went on to talk about the dangers and the lack of safety. Safety, he explained, is not economical and since the plant is a commercial operation, the company, any company, will spend as little as is legally possible. It is up to the NRC to demand strict safety standards. But the NRC is not doing that. It doesn't want to make a wave. He explained what happened at the Fukushima and why the same thing could happen at Pilgrim. The Mark I design at the plant is the same as Fukushima. The containment design was bad when they built Pilgrim. The possible loss of off- site power had not been accounted for. The emergency planning for evacuation or for staying in place is not adequate. The cables were not built for dampness;

the buried cables are corroding and there is no way to check where the worst rusting is taking place. They are not prepared for power outages. There need to be adequate generators to keep the reactors cool. The spent rods, since we now realize will not find a home in Nevada or most likely anywhere else, need to be safely stored in dry casks at the plant. Presently they are shoved together into wet pools — over 3000 of them into storage meant for 800.

Helen, Ann and Sarah listened. They were aware that Ben knew what he was talking about. Ben had always been a supporter of nuclear power. He had seen it as the only way to stop using fossil fuels, depending on oil from the middle-east and on coal with its contaminating smoke stacks and mine disasters. Yet he maintained that the plant was unsafe. Ben wanted to move away, sell the Compound and take the cash to buy a substantial house for his expanding family.

Sarah understood the issues. She'd been working in the environmental field for over ten years. She and Bob often talked about his work with the town; he was trying to get the owners of the power plant to address safety issues and he pushed the town to be tougher with the plant and with NRC. She needed to get away from the horror of Bob's declining health and all it implied. The town and the Compound held no joy for her anymore. When he recovered their plan was to move to her apartment in Boston.

Helen and Ann were still clinging to the hope that if you planted enough trees around the edges of the property and turned off all communication, inside the compound, nothing bad from outside would seep in. Life could be lived as it was in their childhood.

Ben pushed them to make a decision. Did they want to put the Compound on the market, take the money and either buy another place or divide the proceeds among themselves?

Helen and Ann voted not to sell. Sarah and Ben voted to sell. "Well then, we have to call Harry to cast the deciding vote," Ben announced.

He called Harry after they left. "Harry, how are things? I understand you've got a new posting to the Embassy in Paris. Good work!"

"I'll be the lowest of the low at the Embassy. But that has its advantages. Almost no representation duties will be required, meaning that we won't need to entertain and be entertained. Our evenings will be free. We will have more time to ourselves and Paris will be our playground. What's up? I hope nothing's wrong. Is my father OK?"

"He's still hanging in. What an amazing constitution he has. He's refused food and medications, as you know, for the last week. But his great bountiful heart keeps ticking. What I'm calling about is the fate of the Compound. Remember, we set Labor Day as day for the final decision about the Compound. We had a meeting last night at my office and even managed to take a straw vote in between the usual chatter, gossip and menus for dinner. Sarah and I vote to look into selling the place. We believe the Compound is simply not working. The taxes and other expenses are too high, the power plant too threatening. Sarah is a mess about Bob. She wants nothing to do with Plymouth. Natalie and I had hoped to fix up the Portable for year round living, but that's not in the cards. So, I'd like out. I propose we sell the Compound and split the proceeds. Ann and Helen want to hang on at all costs. They claim there's nothing like it anywhere else and feel that it is important in many and varied ways. I could go on, but what it comes down to is your vote. We need to break the tie. How do you feel about it? Do you want to sell out or do you want to keep it?"

There was a long pause. Finally, Ben said, "Harry, are you there?"

"Yeah, I'm here. But I don't know what to say. Of course I want to keep it, but I have little to offer in the short term. The money would be nice if we sell, but I'm not sure I want that money. It's sort of dirty money selling out our birthright and it's a awful thing to do to our sisters who have good reasons to keep the place. I don't know. In fact, I just can't deal with thinking about it now. We're coming up tomorrow for Labor Day and through the wedding. I'll try to have an answer then."

"What is the date of the wedding?"

"It's on Sunday, September 11 at ten in the morning. We sent you the invitation. Didn't you get it?"

"Are you kidding? That's the tenth anniversary of the nine eleven attacks."

"Oh. I hadn't thought of that. Does it matter?"

"They are predicting terrorist activities around the world to mark the occasion. We've had warnings here about the nuclear power plant. We're already on high alert."

Ann pulled Helen aside when they returned to the Compound after the meeting. "Can you spare a few minutes? I'd like to talk with you."

"Sure. Let's go for a drink at Berts." The road outside the driveway to the Compound was jammed with traffic. People were gearing up for the Labor Day weekend, stocking up on food, doing the last of the back to school shopping.

They found a table by the window at the bar. Helen ordered a vodka tonic. "Lemonade for me," Ann said to the waiter. She looked at Helen. "I guess you haven't noticed. I don't want to make a big deal of it, but I'm not drinking. I stopped the morning after the last get together, the so-called part 2 of the annual meeting. It was a bad night for me. If you didn't know, I tripped and fell on the stairs, yelled at the kids and berated my mother. Frank told me I was a mess."

"I'll admit I heard rumors."

"The next morning, paying for my sins with a colossal headache, I called Anita and asked her to take me to a meeting. I felt like hell, was ashamed, and when I saw myself in the mirror I practically fainted. I'd been thinking about it for quite a while, like every hung-over morning, but it took that shameful night with all the Big House listening to make me go through with it. There's an early morning group that meets in a church basement. I'm usually back home before anyone is up or knows I'm gone. Which is good. It's not that I mind if people know I'm an alcoholic, but I'd like to get a few weeks of sobriety under my belt first."

"That's great, Ann. I know it's not easy, especially at first. If I'd known I wouldn't have ordered a drink."

"It doesn't bother me. And I want to keep it that way. I'd rather not abandon my drinking friends. Some people can drink, some can't, I'm in the latter category."

"As far as other people's opinions you shouldn't worry. I've seen this happen with friends. They stumble around drunk and make fools of themselves, yet they think for some reason that this behavior is better in the eyes of their friends than actually admitting they have a problem and sobering up."

"I guess you're right. It doesn't make sense. But I wanted to let you know. Having the possibility of going in with you on a Le Brunch is the thing that keeps me going. That and the humor at the meetings."

"I hope we'll do the restaurant together. I need moral support too. It's been a lonely, unstable few months for me. It'll be fun to make plans together. I've decided to set up an office at the Incubator until we get under way. And I'm looking for a house to rent downtown for the winter. We can talk about where we want to locate the restaurant. It doesn't need to be Plymouth.

Ann gulped her lemonade and ordered another. "You've lost weight," she said. Are you all right?"

"Come on, Ann. You know I was too fat. I made up my own diet, of sorts, just cutting out breads and dessert for the past two months. I hope I can keep it off. Let's sit down next week after Labor Day when the kids are in school and start making plans. Meanwhile, jot down any ideas that pop into your head. This is going to be good. It'll keep our minds off booze and philandering husbands."

Fifteen

"Thanks for meeting us, Mum. I know how you hate airport pick-ups." Harry gave his mother a quick kiss on the right cheek. She gave him one in return on the left. "You must start practicing the both cheek kissing before Paris."

"Hello Mrs. Lloyd," Peter held out his hand.

"Please call me Kitty." She refused his hand and gave him double cheek kisses. "We're all very excited about the wedding."

"How's Dad?" Harry asked.

"Still among the living. I know he wants to see you before he dies and you have probably made it just in time. I'd be with him now but I wanted to talk to Charlie about some legal stuff before the weekend. I've been staying at the apartment for a couple of days."

Peter said, "I'm afraid this is an awkward time for our wedding."

"Don't give it another thought. Paul would be devastated if he thought his death was disrupting anything."

Peter looked uncomfortable and began moving the bags into the car.

"You'll have to get used to her," Harry said. "She and my father have weird ideas about propriety and the afterlife and just about everything else."

"Call it weird if you must, but it works for us."

Paul was spending his last days in bed. He was weak; it was uncomfortable to be moved to a chair. The team of helpers, by now they were his friends, kept a close eye and came into his room with kind words and gentle touches. But they sensed his withdrawal and were careful not to be intrusive on what they now realized was his active internal intellectual and spiritual life. Even the hospice people did not overplay their care. In conversations earlier with Kitty, they were told that the family had thoroughly discussed end of life issues and did not need a lot of moral support; she said they were uncomfortable talking about their private beliefs.

Well, God, here I am. Another day has dawned and I'm still here. This is the day the lord has made, let us rejoice and be glad in it. And so I am. I am glad for all I have been given. I am even thankful for these last months with time for reflection. I like lying here remembering the good times – and the bad times as well. My years at Lisburn had their frustrations, but helping the boys through puberty and watching them make their way in the world was satisfying. I don't hear from them much, but that's normal. I hear about them, or read about them in the news. I'm pretty sure I made a difference in their lives and perhaps more importantly, took some of the pressures off the parents. Parents always forget what it was like to be a teenager. They hover over and try to control their children and then feel they've done a bad job when the teenagers rebel testing their wings. I always advised the parents of naughty boys to give them a long but firm leash. I'd offer up a pithy quotation from the Bible or Shakespeare to make my point. Nothing changes. There's always some quotation that fits. Kitty, too, loved living at the school and being the mother of house mothers par excellence. Of course she can't help continuing the job now at the Compound. It's in her bones. But the children—ours and Parker's—let her have her way. Especially now, with me like this, they feel she needs occupational therapy. There's no better therapy for Kitty than taking charge plus doing most of the heavy work. She told me once that she gets great pleasure washing windows. She loves shoveling manure and cutting brush. It never fails to surprise people when they catch such a feminine beauty out doing the hard labor. Good for her, it costs a fortune to hire anyone. I still wonder if she was there when the tree fell on me. I don't remember a thing, even for days before and after it happened. I'm not so sure Ann and Harry loved their life on campus. Growing up at Lisburn with me as head was awkward for them. I had the feeling that Harry often felt I spent more time with the other boys, that I didn't relate as well to him and his interests as I did to the football and hockey players. Probably true, but he was always different. I'm not sure I could have done anything to ease him through those years even if we didn't live on campus. Ann was always getting chased by the boys. I suppose we could have sent her away to boarding school, but we would have missed her badly, especially Kitty. Well, I'm off the subject here, God. But I'm hoping you listen to my thoughts and find a place for me in one of your many mansions. I know there are things I have left undone and things I shouldn't have done. Please forgive me. I'm hoping things will go well for the family; that the nuclear power plant threat will go away so that people won't have to live in fear. The only thing to fear is fear itself, to paraphrase FDR.

I'm tired and ready move on.

Back in the Compound, the youngsters had tied balloons to trees along the driveway and hung a banner they'd painted on an old sheet: <u>Welcome Home Harry and Peter</u>. Kitty smiled as she drove in. How great to be young and without prejudice. It doesn't occur to children to wonder about a man marrying a man. Older generations learn by being around younger ones, just as much as the young learn from their elders. Their innocent fresh faces and honest comments override questions and uncomfortable feelings the so-called mature members of the family have about this wedding. They had formed a parade to march the couple into the house led by a band made up of trumpet, a pot beaten with a wooden spoon, the ukulele, her old recorder, cymbals of two pan covers. The tune was not recognizable but it was a loud and cheery procession. Harry jumped out of the car and, doing a buck and wing, followed the parade to the house. The dogs yipped and jumped around them. Peter grabbed his suitcase and danced along behind. Kitty could see he loved the welcome; she turned the car around and drove out to Brewster House.

"So here we are Peter," Harry said. "The guest house is ours through the wedding. I'm afraid this family may be more than you bargained for. Don't worry, there aren't always so many brats underfoot. One of the nephews invited three of his classmates to visit for the weekend before school starts. There won't be this many kids at the wedding."

"I adore it. You're lucky you have such a big family. I wish I did."

"Well, you do now—or will in a little over a week. Get yourself settled, then join us on the banking for a drink."

Greg met Kitty at Brewster House door. "Glad you're here. I don't think he'll last much longer. He is waiting for you."

Paul died ten minutes after she sat down beside his bed.

She stayed on at Brewster House, comfortable in the atmosphere and the company of Paul's many friends, both staff and inmates. She was in no rush to return to the Compound and break the news while the family were welcoming Peter and talking about wedding plans. She had already made preliminary arrangements with the undertaker; he needed only a quick call. Everything was in order. Yet. . . for all the months of preparation, for all her understanding and acceptance, Paul's death hit her hard. She crumpled into a soft chair in the small sitting room across from Paul's room, as if she'd been punched in the belly and pushed down. She pounded her fists on the arms of the chair, then hung her head in her hands and sobbed.

"Are you all right? Do you want company?" Greg stood at the door.

"Thanks, no. Just leave me alone for a while."

Peter joined Harry and his family on the banking and introduced himself to Helen, Sarah, Ben and Natalie, Ann and Frank. While he shook hands all around, Harry fixed him a rum and tonic.

"Harry started to fill us in on the wedding plans," Ann said to Peter. "Sounds nice— the ceremony at sea and the party here afterward. Hope the weather holds."

"We've ordered a tent haven't we, Harry?"

"Yes, that's all set. Moveable Feast will do the catering. We'll be going down to talk to them next Tuesday. Lizzie wants to do the photos. She's quite a budding photographer for just fourteen. So far we have about seventy-five acceptances."

"Who's coming?" Helen asked.

"A lot of our friends from Washington you don't know. Peter's mother and father. All of you guys, of course, plus kids and dogs. The uncles have regretted. Not that I expected John, though I thought he just might come east before Dad kicks the bucket. I'm sad that Uncle Parker and Aunt Priscilla can't come. Yeah I know they were just here and it's a long drive, but still . . . they practically raised me and . . . "

"Oh that's outrageous," Helen interrupted. "I'm going to call them."

"No, don't," Harry advised. "They have their reasons and we understand. Not everyone is comfortable yet or accepts same sex marriage."

"Dear Mater and Pater will be the last," Sarah said.

Ben turned to her and said quietly, "Take it easy on them; they're doing the best they can."

"How come you're suddenly so big and beautiful? What's gotten into you? The last time we were together you were furious at all of us for not making a decision. Why haven't you gotten Harry's vote by now?"

"Be quiet, Sarah. He just got here. We'll talk about it tomorrow."

The sun was going down – a large orange orb sinking into the water. Shades of orange, red, and pink painted patterns in the western sky and were reflected in the calm ocean below. A good omen to welcome Peter into the family. Mosquitoes, arriving on cue as soon as the sun disappeared, were chased by dragon flies. The Lloyds reveled in this natural mosquito control program.

They moved inside to the dining room for the traditional dinner to welcome guests: steamed clams, lobsters and corn, followed by pie and ice cream. Table talk was lively with wedding plans, jokes, reminiscences, laughter.

Kitty walked in as they were finishing the dishes. There was no hiding her news. Moving into the living room they, talked about Paul. First quietly and sadly then telling stories, laughing. Peter said, "I'm sorry not to have gotten to know him."

"At least you had a chance to meet before the accident. He was very impressed," Kitty told him.

Harry said, "I'm upset that I didn't go down with you to see him. I had no idea he'd die today. I just wasn't thinking. As usual, I was thinking only of myself."

"Don't say that, Harry. I told him you had just flown in from Washington and that you would be along any minute. He knew you'd want to settle in at home and introduce Peter to the gang first."

The next morning, Sarah drove to Brewster House. She walked past Paul's empty room to number 12 at the end of the corridor. "So here you are!" she said. "I hope you don't mind being in with all the old crocks, but it was the only bed we could find in town. Greg took you in as a special favor."

"I figured it was something like that."

"I just wanted to tell you that Uncle Paul died last night."

"Oh, I am so sorry. What a great loss to the world. Please extend my condolences and love to your family."

"Thanks. I will. Of course it was not unexpected, but still it's hard."

"It must be. How's your aunt doing?"

"She's not taking it well. We're all surprised to see she's not as stoic as we thought. They loved each other very much. You look much better. How was the trip down from Boston?"

"Pretty strange lying flat out in an ambulance in the middle of Labor Day weekend traffic to the Cape. Thank goodness they didn't put the sirens on. It was a parking lot on Route Three. I'm glad to be back in Plymouth; I didn't have much fun at the rehab place in Boston. I feel like shit. I feel as if I've been run over by a Mac truck. I can hardly lift my arm."

Sarah kissed his cheek and told him he looked just wonderful to her.

That night, Sarah invited all the kids to sleep with her in the Portable. Helen had moved out to stay with Kitty, who had moved into the Big House with Ann and Frank so that Harry and Peter could have the Guest House. Changing beds was something the Lloyds were used to.

They played badminton on the scruffy Portable lawn until mosquitoes drove them inside. After cooking pop corn and fudge, they chose sides for charades. This was therapy for Sarah, taking her mind off Bob. He just didn't seem to be getting any better.

It was past midnight before the gang of nieces and nephews were finally asleep and crammed into the bunk rooms close to the living room. She slept in the big bedroom down the hall. She woke up suddenly, hearing the front door open. Who could it be? They never locked the doors. Half of them didn't even close There was no dog in the house, no dog to warn of strangers. . She stayed in bed, pulling the covers up to her neck, ashamed of being such a coward, but too frightened to move.

"Sarah. Could you come out to the living room? I need to talk with you."

Oh, thank goodness, she thought, it's Frank. She stuck her feet into slippers, pulled on her white terrycloth beach robe and shuffled out to talk to her cousin's husband.

"What is it, Frank?"

"It's about Bob. "

"Oh no. What?"

"Dr. Patel called."

"Did he tell you what's wrong. He's so weak."

"Patel is now considering that your fears of poisoning may have feet. They did more testing and had him under close observation for these past few weeks. They can't figure out any other possibility."

"I knew it. No one would listen. Well now we know what it is at least. What's the plan?"

"Well, this is the problem Sarah. The poison has done a job on Bob. His kidneys, his liver and all his vital organs are weakened, weakened beyond repair. That's why they sent him back to Plymouth, so at least he can be closer to his family – and to you."

Sarah paled. "No! No, I won't accept that. Move him back to Mass General. Get him out of the nursing home. They can do something in Boston."

"Patel has been talking with Bob's family. It is really up to them."

"I'll talk to Bob. He's a fighter."

"Well that's what I have to tell you. Bob's slipped into a coma. They've taken him over to Jordan Hospital. Brewster House doesn't have the facilities to deal with his current state. He's in ICU at Jordan. I'm afraid it really doesn't look good."

Early the next morning Sarah drove to the hospital. She left a note on the kitchen table telling the still sleeping children to go to the Big House for breakfast.

When she got to the hospital, she told the unattached voice answering the bell at the locked Intensive Care Unit that she wanted to visit Bob Meyer.

"He's gone," was the reply.

"What room is he in?" she asked. There was a pause.

"Please wait, someone will be right out."

"What do you mean?! Of course he didn't die. Where is he?" Sarah screamed at the nurse.

"Are you a family member?"

"I'm his girlfriend." As soon as she said it she realized how unimportant and insignificant she sounded.

"I'm truly sorry for your loss. But I'm afraid I can't say more, I suggest you call his family."

Sarah was shivering and felt faint. She found a seat in the small waiting room outside the ICU and tried to pull herself together. After a few minutes she got up and stumbled out of the unit. She stopped at the chapel. But she didn't know how to pray or what to do. She stared at the non denominational purple velvet curtain in front of her. She checked her watch. Seven thirty. She needed to find Bob. Was he in the hospital morgue or at an undertaker's? Confused and dazed, she left the chapel and wandered the hospital's baffling hallways. Wings and additions had been attached to the original nineteenth century federal style building through the years, according to architectural fashion of the day but with no thought to reason or ease of traffic flow. A nurse stopped her and asked if she could help.

" I'm trying to find Bob Meyers. He just died."

"Are you a family member?"

"I'm his fiancée," she upgraded.

"I'm afraid the hospital can't tell you anything. You'll have to call his family."

"Would he be in the morgue or something?"

"I just don't know, and even if I did I wouldn't be able to say."

"But he has no family nearby," Sarah lied.

"You might speak with the head of social services. She'll be able to help." The nurse gave directions.

Sarah wondered off dazed with sadness, anger, and confusion. She found an exit, went to the parking lot and sat in her car. She stared into space, trying to focus on what to do but was too distraught to make a decision.

Frank found her an hour later. "Sarah, I was just going inside to talk with the staff when I saw you here. Why don't I drive you home first?"

"Your didn't tell me he was dead."

"You weren't really hearing me last night. I told you he was dying, but you didn't want to believe it –

understandably. He died at three this morning. The hospital just called me because I was his admitting doctor."

"He's dead."

"You should go home and get some rest."

"No. I am going to the Meyers to be with his family. I want to be sure we follow up on who poisoned him."

"We need to talk about this," Frank saw she was in shock. "I suggest you come inside and have breakfast in the cafeteria while I talk with hospital staff."

Sarah followed him to the cafeteria. By the time Frank joined her she had pulled herself together enough to begin forming a plan. "We need to be sure they do an autopsy on Bob to figure out what killed him. We need to find out who wanted to shut him up. We need to make sure the murderer is tried and put away."

"Bob's family has already had the body removed by the funeral home. They will be burying him within twenty-four hours, according to Jewish law, or tradition anyway. There will be no autopsy. The family's wishes in a case like this overrule the medical establishment recommendations."

"Well then I'm going to talk to the family right now and explain things to them. I know Bob would want this to be investigated."

"That would be very stupid. For one thing it's too late, for another you would be interfering with their mourning and their traditions."

"What about my mourning? We were practically engaged. I was closer to Bob than most of his family. They won't miss him like I do." Frank convinced her to wait a few hours at least.

When she got back to the Compound, Sarah walked up the path to the Portable. She stood for a few minutes like a zombie in the middle of the living room. Slowly she pushed aside flip flops, a teddy bear, goggles, the jack of hearts and a Red Sox tee shirt; she lay down and stretched out on the chintz covered sofa. Pop corn was strewn on the floor along with crumpled pieces of paper, the discarded charades to act out. Sarah glanced at the mess without interest; tried to sleep but sleep did not come. The others were at the Big House or on the beach. She was too restless for sleep and thought of joining them. But they would be making plans, talking about the wedding and, of course, Paul.

Indeed they were. Harry was furious when his mother suggested that they have Paul's funeral the day after the wedding to make double use of the tent. "She's such a cheapskate," he said, and apologized to Peter for her rude behavior. It would be totally inappropriate for them and their guests to know there was to be a funeral the very next day in the very same place as the wedding. Peter disagreed. He thought it was perfectly logical and even suggested that any food leftover from the wedding could be served the next day at the funeral. Kitty was delighted to hear that Peter's outlook on life appeared to agree with her own. Another advantage, Kitty suggested, was that many of the same people would be coming to both events and could spend the night.

"Events!" Harry had screamed. "You can't be serious, Mother. Our wedding and Dad's funeral aren't events like football games or rock concerts. They are important life defining ceremonies that should stand alone and be honored."

Kitty apologized and before returning to the Big House, asked Harry to make a few calls to let close friends know about Paul before they saw the obituary in the newspaper. Harry and Peter had been given special dispensation from Kitty; they were allowed cell phones so Harry could keep in touch with the State Department as his orders to Paris were being processed.

Peter asked Harry to fill him in on a few things he didn't understand. "What," he asked, "did Ben and Sarah mean about a making a decision and casting a vote? Why is he so sensitive to his mother's seemingly reasonable suggestion about tent sharing? Why was Ann so quiet, where was Helen's husband, when is Sarah's baby due?"

"It's been a terrible summer here. It's usually quiet and relaxed and we feel we are in the middle of nowhere. Normally, we keep the world at bay and depend only on each other and our few friends; we read, play games, talk, eat, sleep. But this year has been nuts. Of course the aftermath of my father's accident has been a sad steady drone. His living on in a vegetative state has been hard on everyone. But the biggest disturbance to our halcyon days, our New England style Brigadoon, has been the new awareness of the nuclear power plant; the fears that a disaster such as Fukushima could happen here. My cousin Sarah understands the issues and is worried; but she is distraught because her boyfriend is at death's door and she thinks he was poisoned. She wants to sell the Compound. The Compound is in the hands of my sister and I and our three cousins; we five are called the ruling generation. My mother has a hard time giving up control and we've been humoring her since my father's accident. She is adamant that we keep this place. She thinks nothing is more important than family and especially this type of communal living with generations interacting. Ben wants to sell the Compound as he needs the money for a house of his own; he too is concerned about the nuclear power plant. Ann and Helen want to hang on, in spite of the plant's proximity. I have promised to cast the deciding vote (to sell or not to sell that is the question) before Labor Day. As for the rest of your questions: Helen's husband stayed in Paris this year; word is it's a trial separation. Ann has recently given up drinking; she's a bit grumpy. Natalie's baby is due in mid September, but if you ask me it'll pop any day. What a pain it all is. We should have held the wedding somewhere else, especially now that Dad's funeral is upon us. It's not that I'm selfish, but I do feel that the focus should be on us."

"I see your point, but I don't agree. I hope your vote will be not to sell. You were here – your family was here – before the power plant. Why should you be the ones to move? You have no idea how lucky all of you are to have such a place. My parents are in one of those sterile "retirement communities". It's a ghetto made up of people of a certain age and economic income. There are no children, no dogs, no cats. Everything is neat and clean, the inmates well groomed, the lawns tidy, the flowers lined up in rows. I support your mother's view. Surely you want to keep this property so that when we have home leave or vacation we can come and join the fun and the fights. I understand the fears one might feel living next to a nuclear plant. But I'm not sure you can feel safe anywhere in this old world. Who would have thought there would be an earthquake in Virginia this week big enough to shake us up in Washington. Natural disasters are everywhere, as are man-made ones. What about the nut case shooting people at a camp in Norway of all places? Disasters happen everywhere. You should cling to this land and you should cling to each other—and I mean the whole family. I love this family of yours. What a surprising extra benefit I get marrying you.

"Hey. . . I've just had a great idea", Peter continued. "I could help organize a major initiative to have the power plant made safe. I could research nuclear plants in France, of which there are many. I can write articles for the magazine; they have suggested a few topics for me but have also asked me to come up with my own ideas. I could write an article comparing the plants in France to the ones in the U.S. and I could write interesting human interest pieces about people's reactions: French and American. Sarah and I can correspond on ways to ensure that Pilgrim is safe. Major publicity is important to get the public involved and to get the politicians on board. Never underestimate the power of the pen. And as you know I have a powerful pen."

"Good luck, Peter. I don't want to discourage you, but it's been tried before. Groups form, small demonstrations and meetings take place. The press gets on it and for a while the public is pulled out of its lethargy, petitions are written and there is a small spark of interest. But then, just as it looks as if an organized effort will form, some distraction rears up. People are busy; they are fickle. But don't let that hold you back. It's a wonderful idea. And thanks for the vote of support for this nut case family. I can see you'll fit right in."

"I'm going to the beach and a walk around the Compound. I might bump into Sarah and talk with her about the idea."

Messages were being passed around the country on facebook and by emails asking people to show the American flag on September eleven. The power plant was testing the emergency warning system more often. The Lloyds ignored it all.

Kitty sat on the Big House porch and with yellow legal pad and pen was compiling to do lists for the coming week and for the funeral. Ann and Helen were with her sipping iced tea and offering help. Natalie was asleep in the hammock. She was huge and looked ready to produce. "Where's Frank," Kitty asked her daughter.

"He's with Sarah visiting Bob," Ann replied. "Apparently they took him to the hospital from Brewster House last night. I don't think it's serious. I hope not."

"Poor Sarah. She's going through a lot. I hope Bob pulls through. It's been a long haul. Almost two months since he collapsed in the outside shower. It's made her very jumpy," Kitty said. "Now I must get back to my lists. I'm held up on many things until we can choose a date for the funeral. Harry is so stubborn about our not having it in the same tent as the wedding. Maybe if I offer two days in between events – oops I mean between 'life defining ceremonies', as Harry calls them. We could have the funeral on Tuesday. Tuesday is a funereal kind of day. Having the wedding and the funeral close means that those who come from afar can take in both. Like Parker and Priscilla. I understand they regretted the wedding invite. But surely they'll come for Paul; they will then be captured for the wedding. Now, what else do I need to do? As soon as we know the date, I'll call the church, the minister, the organist, the Lisburn a capella group. Oh yes, we need to get the obit in the paper. But I have to know the funeral date for that too. I'm not going to have it catered. Much more fun to make stuff ourselves and include a pot luck. People always bring covered dishes in Plymouth. Frank and Ben can tend bar."

"Mother, you should spring for a caterer so you don't have to worry about food."

"Nonsense. Caterers would make it too formal."

"I'll take care of the food," Helen said. "It is my trade, after all. What I'll do is oversee the works. I'll use leftovers from the wedding, accept the covered dishes and add some Le Brunch specialties. The children will help."

"Oh that's perfect dear. Thank you."

Ann said, "I'm going over to the guest house to talk with Harry and Peter. I'll lie if necessary and tell them that Tuesday is the only day the minister can make it."

Kitty said, "We'll fling his ashes to sea. We can all go down after the funeral and get the flotilla into the water. Canoe, kayaks, row boat, the little sail boat. I picture us dumping the ashes in the spot where Paul caught the big striper a couple of years ago. He'll love it."

Made in the USA
Charleston, SC
05 December 2011